IN THIS FAR-FUTURE ADVENTURE
EXTRAVAGANZA ABOUT A MERCENARY ARMY
OF RARE ABILITIES, JOEL ROSENBERG HAS
CAPTURED THE MARTIAL SPIRIT OF ITS
THRILLING GALAXY-WIDE CAMPAIGNS.

NOT FOR GLORY

"SUPERB . . . COMPELLING . . . INTRIGUING . . .
it has the feel of reality and life . . . truly outstanding
. . . I loved it!"
—John Dalmas, author of *The Reality Matrix*

"Joel Rosenberg has taken some tried-and-true elements
of military science fiction and breathed new life into
them with intelligence and superb characterizations. AN
ORIGINAL AND POWERFUL BOOK!"
—Roland J. Green, author of *The Peace Company*

"Joel Rosenberg knows how to handle mayhem . . . a
well-crafted reminder of wars' one true purpose."
—Analog Science Fiction/Science Fact

"Skillful and entertaining . . . The combination of action
and tactics keeps the plot rolling."
—*Cincinatti Post*

D0191533

NOT FOR GLORY

JOEL ROSENBERG

A SIGNET BOOK

NEW AMERICAN LIBRARY

for Bob Adams

Not for Glory previously appeared in an NAL BOOKS edition published
by New American Library and published simultaneously in Canada
by The New American Library Limited.

 SIGNET TRADEMARK REG. U.S. PAT. OFF. AND FOREIGN COUNTRIES
REGISTERED TRADEMARK—MARCA REGISTRADA
HECHO EN CHICAGO, U.S.A.

SIGNET, SIGNET CLASSIC, MENTOR, ONYX, PLUME, MERIDIAN
and NAL BOOKS are published by NAL PENGUIN INC.,
1633 Broadway, New York, New York 10019

First Signet Printing, March, 1989

1 2 3 4 5 6 7 8 9

PRINTED IN THE UNITED STATES OF AMERICA

Acknowledgments

I'm indebted to the people who helped me both with and through the writing of this one: my wife, Felicia, for reasons obvious and obscure; John M. Ford, for the title; John F. Carr, who encouraged me to continue the Metzada stories; Harry F. Leonard, Second Lieutenant, Connecticut National Guard (Retired), for his usual quibbling as well as invaluable help with the military aspects of the book; my editor, John Silbersack; and, most particularly, my new agent, Eleanor Wood.

A special mention is due my copyeditor, Mark J. McGarry, whose efforts and suggestions went above and beyond what's normally expected of a copyeditor, much to the betterment of the work.

Metzada, noun—

1. (archaic) An ancient rock fortress in the Palestine satrapy of Great Persia, about twenty kilometers south of En Gedi. Scene, circa 72-73 A.D., of the final stand of Jewish zealots against Rome; the defenders killed themselves rather than surrender.
2. The second planet of Epsilon Indi, inhabited primarily by descendants of Jewish refugees from the State of Israel and the North American Federation. Metzada's only significant commercial export is the sale of the services of the Metzadan Mercenary Corps.
3. Colloquial for the Metzadan Mercenary Corps.

PROLOGUE: CINCINNATUS

The log cabin was drafty and cold; I moved a bit closer to the stove, and took a deep draft from the stone tankard. It was real Earth coffee, black and rich.

The old man chuckled, as though over some private joke.

"What the hell is so funny?" I didn't bother to keep the irritation out of my voice. It had taken me more than seven hundred hours to reach Thellonee and then to travel west from New Portsmouth first by rail, then skimmer, and finally on foot to reach Shimon Bar-El's cabin, and every time I'd try to bring up the reason I'd come from Metzada, the old bastard would just chuckle and change the subject, ask me about my wives, or about a cousin, or about how Dov was doing, as though to tell me we'd discuss business at his pleasure, not mine.

"You are what is so funny, Tetsuo. Tetsuki. Nephew." Bar-El sat back in his chair, shaking his head. He set his mug down, and then rubbed at his eyes with arthritis-swollen knuckles.

"Damn these hands," he said. He picked up his mug and

drained it. "May have to go back to civilization to have them treated." He set the mug down on the rough-hewn table, and rubbed his eyes again. It's always seemed to me to be kind of strange: I bear the name of one of our Nipponese ancestors— Tetsuo Imaoka, my many-times-great grandfather—but Shimon has the epicanthic folds. Me, I look almost Aryan.

"And why am I so funny, Uncle?" *You traitorous bastard.*

There isn't a nastier word in the language than "traitor." Metzada relies on credits we earn offworld, and that depends in large part on our reputation. No, that's too cold, too complicated. Simply: if nobody will pay Metzada to fight, my children will not eat.

There hadn't been proof that Shimon Bar-El had taken a payoff on Oroga; had there been, he would have been hanged in disgrace, not merely cashiered and exiled.

Although ... the argument could be made that hanging would have been kinder—but never mind that. The suspicion, combined with what little evidence I could put together, had been enough to strip him of rank and citizenship.

I would have given a lot if we didn't need him now.

"Well," he said, "you've been here all day and you haven't asked me if I really did take that payoff."

He cocked his head to one side, his eyes going vague. "I can remember when that was of some importance to you, *Inspector*-General." The accent on "inspector" was a dig. Unlike Shimon Bar-El, I've always been a staff officer; the only way I could get stars was to become the IG—there simply isn't another general in Metzada who doesn't command fighting forces.

"I ... don't really care. Not anymore," I lied. I had trouble getting the next words out. But I did. It was my job. I'm very good at doing my job. "Because we've come up with a way for you to earn your way home."

He raised an eyebrow. "I doubt that. You've never understood me, Tetsuo Hanavi, have you?"

I shrugged. "Maybe not."

"I can read you like a book," he said. "There's a contract that's come up, right?"

"Yes, and—"

"Yes, and shut up while I'm speaking. I'm still your uncle, boy. I want to show you how well I know you. It's on a low-tech world, correct?"

I shrugged. Not impressive. "That's your specialty, isn't it?"

"One of them." He smiled. "So why do I think I'm so smart, eh? Let me tell you more about the contract. It's high pay, and it's tough, and it looks like there's no way to do whatever the locals are paying Metzada to do."

I nodded. "Right. Right now we're short of low-tech specializing generals. Gevat is off on Schriftalt; Abromovitz, Alon, and Cohen are bogged down on Rand."

He shrugged. "If it was up to me, I'd just give your brother his stars and let him take it."

"Not possible. He only got his second leaf last year, and, besides, he got hurt on Rand."

Concern creased his face. "Ari's hurt? How bad?"

"Not too. He took a Jecty arrow in the liver. It's taking a while to regenerate, but he'll make it."

He nodded. "Good. A good man, your brother. Too good to be wasted on a useless MG exercise like putting down the peon revolts." Bar-El snorted. "Did you know that Rand was settled by a bunch of idiots who wanted to get away from any kind of government?"

I didn't, actually. I'd just assumed that the feodacracy there had always been there. Ancient history bores me, unless it's my people's history. "No. But we're getting off the subject." I spread my hands. "The point is, you're the only one who's ever generaled this low-tech a campaign who's available."

He pulled a pack of tabsticks from his pocket, and offered one to me before thumbing one to life himself. "*If* I'm available."

I thumbed mine, and waited for the flame to die before I took a deep pull of the rich Thellonee tobacco. They grow some fine tobacco in the New Britain colony. We don't have such things in Metzada; it's one of my guilty pleasures when I'm offworld.

"What's in it for me?" he asked.

I tapped my chest pocket. "I've got a Writ of Citizenship here. If you can salvage the situation, you can go home." I waved my hand around the room. "Unless you like it here better." A battered iron stove stood in the corner, stove-lengths of rough wood piled next to it; next to it was the sleeping area on the dirty, unfinished wood floor. Beyond the sleeping area was the pantry, where a leg of some smoked beast, sliced to white bone on one side, hung from a hook.

By the door a flintlock rifle stood, waiting. You find a lot of flintlock rifles when you get away from civilization. Black powder is cheaper than smokeless powder, and flints, while not easy to find and chip into a useful form, are something you can make yourself—not so for cartridge ammunition, or even percussion caps.

It was kind of sad, really. Shimon Bar-El, who had once commanded armies, reduced to using a muzzle-loader to hunt for his supper.

He sat silently for a long moment, sipping at his coffee, pulling at his tabstick. "You got my commission in another pocket?"

"A temporary commission, yes. I'm not offering to have you permanently reinstated, *traitor*."

"Ah. Good." Shimon Bar-El smiled. "Good. At last you're being honest. Who's the employer?"

"The lowlanders on—"

"Indess. Son of a *bitch*. Rivka manipulated them into asking for me, eh?"

"What do you mean?" He was absolutely right, of course, but there was no way that he could have known that. The deputy premier had kept the negotiations secret; outside of the lowlanders' representatives and my boss, Pinhas Levine, I was the only one who knew how Rivka Effron had suckered them into a payment-under-all-contingencies clause in the contract, conditional only on Shimon Bar-El being in command.

He shrugged. "I know how her mind works. If anyone else were to fail—regardless of what the contract says—it'd be bad for Metzada's reputation. But if they'd asked for Bar-El the

Traitor, demanded him, insisted on him, it'd be on their own heads. Right?"

That was exactly right.

"Of course not," I said.

My orders were specific. Rivka had been sure that he'd work this part of it out, but I wasn't to admit anything. Shimon Bar-El was a sneaky bastard—it was entirely possible that our conversation was being taped, despite the poverty of the surroundings, despite any assurances to the contrary.

Bar-El rose, going to the battered pot on the cast-iron stove, pouring himself another cup of coffee.

"I'll believe what my own mind tells me," he said as he stirred a heaping tablespoon of sugar into the rich black brew, then returned to his seat, sipping. "Good coffee—you want more? No? As I was saying, it's out of the question. I've been thinking of moving back to New Portsmouth and trying to get some more consulting work. But I've no intention of being set up as the sacrificial lamb."

He drained the cup and set it down on the table. "I don't bleat any too well."

"You arrogant bastard." I stood. "You think you're unique, you think that we'll give you a permanent commission if you agree to take this one on?" I picked up my bag. "We're going to take this contract anyway. The offer's just too good to pass up. I'll handle it myself, if I have to."

He snickered at that. "Don't be such an idiot, Tetsuo. Old Rivka wouldn't let you. You don't have any field experience, not in command. A lot of good boys would die, just because—"

"You shut your mouth, traitor. Maybe I don't have any command experience, but almost nobody does, not against cavalry. There hasn't been—"

"Cavalry?"

"Cavalry. You want me to spell it for you?"

There was a strange smile at the edges of his lips, only. "Cavalry. As in horses. On Indess. Only one part of the continent matters; and horses don't swim in the World Sea. Lowlanders trying to take the highlands. Hill country."

He closed his eyes for a moment, then opened them and shook his head. "I don't see the problem. You just set up your pikemen, let them impale the critters against your line. Even if they're using black powder, you stick to bows. Take a bit of discipline, even for Metzadan line troops, to hold the line . . ."

He shrugged. "What am I missing?"

"We're not the good guys, is what you're missing. We're supposed to take a village on Mount Cibo, right smack in the middle of oal country—not that there are a lot of oals left. No meeting engagements—we're going to have to siege. All they have to do is use their cavalry to harass our flanks and we can't get the towers up. Got to use towers—there're no deposits of sulfur available, so there's no gunpowder. Not with what the Commerce Department will let us bring in. Low-tech world, remember?"

"You've got all the tech reports in your bag?"

"Of course I do."

"Then let me see them." He held out a hand. "We're both going to have to study them."

"Both?" I didn't understand. Then again, I've never really understood my uncle.

"Both." He smiled, not pleasantly. "Me, because I'm taking this. And you, because you get to be my aide." He took my bag from me, removed the blue tech report folder, and started spreading papers around on the floor. "We're going to get you some field experience, we are." He studied the sheets silently for a few minutes. "I'll want all the equipment special-ordered, make sure it gets through inspection. You got that, Colonel?"

"Colonel?"

"You just got yourself a negative brevet, nephew. I don't like to see stars on anyone else's shoulders but mine." He picked up a topographical map and spread it out on the floor, then took up a stylus and some paper. "Go take a walk for a few hours, so I can get some work done. I'll have the specs on the equipment in the morning. We're leaving then." He squatted over the topo map. "Cavalry, eh?"

I hadn't gotten used to the three oak leaves of a colonel on my shoulders. Which was kind of silly, really; I'd only been the IG for six months, but I'd put in fifteen years of hard, dirty service earning the IG's stars, and the negative brevet rankled.

The trouble was, of course, that we needed Bar-El, and that meant that I had to put up with whatever indignities he cared to inflict.

For the time being.

I shouldn't complain. Real soldiers risk their lives all too often, openly bearing arms against armed enemies. All I had to do was put up with the sneering of a Thousand Worlds Commerce Department inspector who clearly had no use for Metzada, or for me.

And I had to do it by myself. *General* Bar-El was with the men.

She dumped the contents of the backpack onto the flat black surface of her durlyn desk, the messkit, Fairbairn knife, utility knife, and other items of clothing and equipment falling in agonizing slowness.

"This doesn't look standard," she said, gathering it all into a pile, then picking up the Fairbairn knife, unsheathing it. "I've seen the gear you killers carry before." Inspector Celia von du Mark tested the edge of the blade with her thumbnail. "Molysteel?"

I shook my head. "No, just high-carbon—and no better than they could make down there. The . . . General had everything special-ordered—that's a Fairbairn assault knife. Really more of a dagger. The blade's thin, slips between ribs—"

"Spare me the details, please," she said, tossing her head, sending her shortish black hair whipping around her thin face. "Just as long as you don't violate tech import regs, I don't give a damn what toys you're carrying." Brow furrowed, she cocked her head to one side. "Are you going to claim this is a typical pack?"

I shrugged. "Why not? Check for yourself. We posted bond; we're not going to sacrifice that, not for the sake of having a rustproof knife or two." I sat back in the chair. "But go ahead, have your men—"

"My people."

"—you can have your *animals* check it out for all I care. Except for the medician's kits, the bows, arrows, maps, and the siege-tower cables and hardware, you won't find anything on any of the two thousand men in the regiment that doesn't precisely duplicate what you've got in front of you." I spotted a piece of fur on the corner of her desk, and picked it up. It wasn't prepossessing: just a smooth brown swatch of soft fur, almost the size of my palm. "This is what all the fuss is about?" I sighed. "Doesn't look all that special."

"Try dipping it in a weak solution of acetic acid, and let it dry." She sat down and rummaged in a desk drawer. "Then it looks like this."

A twinkling shape flew toward me; I snatched it out of the air.

Now, this was nice: the swatch was white and shiny, gathering and shattering the light of the overhead glow, a spectrum of color washing over its surface.

"Pretty." I'd never seen a piece of treated oal-fur before; it's strictly a luxury item, and Metzada is a poor world. We have to import all too much; we don't import fur coats. Luxury would be reducing the number of young boys we send offworld to die in other people's wars, not a fur coat for either of my wives.

"What's this?" She held up a folded, triangular piece of fabric, opening it only partway.

"Called a shelter half. It's half a tent; you pitch two of these things face-to-face and you've got room for two soldiers to sleep." I'd asked Shimon why we were taking special-ordered shelter halves, cut and sewn to his design, instead of the usual six-man minitents, and he'd pointed out another use for them. *You can wrap a corpse in one, and bury it deeply,* he'd said. *But don't tell the men. Might make them nervous.* And then he smiled. *I've got one just for you, Tetsuki.*

I fondled the piece of fur. It was nice, certainly, but hardly worth dying for. And, of course, nobody was going to die for fur. The lowlanders were paying us to chase the mountain people out of their walled village halfway up the slopes of Mount Cibo, right in the middle of what was left of oal country, the only remaining area on the planet's single continent where the chipmunk-like creature hadn't been hunted to extinction.

Certainly, some would die. But not for fur. For the credits that keep Metzada alive.

The distinction is important. The distinction is everything.

"And this?" She held up a metal cylinder, flat and half the size of my head.

"That's a messkit, a one-man pressure-cooker. It seals airtight; you put food in, a little water, just chuck it in a fire, leave it for a few minutes, then pull it out with a stick. Then you use the point of your knife to flick that little lever open, releasing the steam. Then open, and eat." I smiled.

She returned my smile. "I've got another use for it. Say, you fill it full of water, bury it in a fire you've built next to a wall—say, a wall around a village on the slopes of Cibo. And then you wait until it builds up enough internal pressure to blow itself apart, and, incidentally, shatter the wall." She tossed the messkit to one side. "Denied. The 'messkits' stay aboard; you and your regiment can skipshuttle down."

I figured a bit of false outrage might go over reasonably. "Inspector, I'll have you know—"

"Enough of that. The Commerce charter provides that offplanet mercenary soldiers can be brought in. Less blood-shed that way, supposedly; I'm not sure. Maybe it's better than letting the locals hack each other to ribbons. But there are limits, and while I'm inspector here they are going to be enforced. Understood?"

I wiped my hand across my forehead. "I know. No import of military—"

"—technology beyond whatever the locals already possess. They don't have bombs like that. They can't make bombs like that. And you can't bring them in. Understood?"

Of course I understood. Shimon should have understood. I'd told him they'd never let us get the messkits by.

We rode down on the first shuttle, along with First Battalion, HQ company and the three battalion commanders, who were also acting as Shimon's general staff, plus their own staffs/bodyguards.

Which was standard—that goes back to the old IDF days, before the exile to Metzada, when none of our soldiers ever set foot on a piece of land where an officer hadn't been first. There's nothing romantic about it, no bravura required—it's just a matter of human economics. We've always had a lot of officer material, and traded off the high mortality among bar-grade and leaf-grade officers for lower casualties among line soldiers.

Other armies did—and still do—see it differently. That's why we're better. And, to a large extent, that's also why I get to wear my stars at home.

I followed Shimon out into the daylight, squinting nervously in the bright sunlight. Indess orbits an F4 star; much brighter, whiter light than we use in Metzada's underground corridors.

15

"Relax," he said, dropping his pack to the tarmac. "We're on Thousand Worlds territory here, in the first place."

Maybe so, but the fence, far off in the distance, looked like it was made of wood—not electrified wire.

We waited while Colonels Davis, Silverstein, and Kaplowitz walked down the ramp, their bodyguards behind them, bows strung and arrows nocked, keeping careful watch on the one-story stone buildings on the south edge of the field. They didn't look any too relaxed.

After them, the rest of headquarters company unloaded, looking more like line soldiers than the clerks and such that kept the regiment running. Shimon beckoned to Natan Raviv, the captain who commanded HQ company, muttered a few words, then sent him and the rest of the company on their way.

The rest of First Battalion quickly unloaded, officers leading their outfits down, until there were more than six hundred men on the tarmac, adjusting their packs and checking over their gear.

"General," I said, "you were saying that the fact that we're on CD territory is in the first place. What's in the second place?"

Shimon Bar-El shrugged. "I doubt that there's a Ciban within a hundred klicks. They're fighting a defensive war, Tetsuo."

He turned. "Yonni, over here," he shouted.

Davis trotted over, his blocky guard behind him. "What is it, Shimon?" Yonaton Davis was a short, wide man, whose girth and blandness always gave me the impression that he was more suited to be a shopkeeper than an officer. I've seen the type before; some compensate by becoming martinets. That's not necessarily wrong, by the way; Eitan was a martinet. So was Patton.

Yonni took the opposite approach, giving and taking orders with an informality that suggested he was good enough, competent enough, not to have to put on airs. Which probably had something to do with why Shimon had made him the regiment's G-3, operations officer, as well as giving him First Battalion.

"Yonni, my aide and I are going to go talk to our employers. Have the staffs and the spearheads and the rest of the stores made ready." He pointed toward the north. "There's an open field there; have your battalion bivouac there, and the other two to your west and east. There won't be any trouble here, but set out a full guard, just for practice."

"I'll set my people to it now, rest of the regiment as soon as they disembark." Davis nodded. "Speaking of practice, though . . ." He bounced on the balls of his feet, experimenting. "We're running a little under nine-tenths of a g here."

"So?"

"So, nobody around here has loosed an arrow under this grav, not recently. You want me to set up some targets, get some practice shooting down?

"No." Shimon Bar-El turned away.

"Wait just a moment, General." Davis reached for his arm, clearly thought better of it, let his hand drop. "They have to get some practice—better here than in combat."

Shimon sighed. "They won't need practice. We're not supposed to win this one." He jerked a thumb at me. "Ask Tetsuo, when we get back. In the meantime, Colonel, just follow orders."

Davis turned away, wordless. I trotted after Shimon.

"What the hell was that for?" I kept my voice calm, with just a touch of tremor for effect.

He snickered. "That's not supposed to be common knowledge, eh? We're supposed to be able to storm a walled city—population about fifteen thousand, three thousand effectives maybe, with two thousand men? While there're horsemen harassing our flanks?"

In fact we weren't supposed to. And we weren't going to. "That's what the contract says."

He patted his hip pocket. "I've got a copy right here. It's handy when you run out of bumwad. Tetsuo, I have no intention of just going through the motions. I'm supposed to fail.

Damned if I'm going to play wargames just to keep you happy."

He looked up at me, a smile quirking across his lips. "But I'll do it to keep our *employer* happy."

At the edge of the field, he stopped a blue-suited Commerce Department stevedore. "How do I go about finding Senhor Felize Regato?"

Regato's mansion was clear evidence that little except military tech was on the proscribed list for Indess. The floors looked to be real Italian marble; among the paintings I spotted a Picasso and a Bartolucci—and the glows overhead made me smile: their light was the same color as the glows at home.

A linen-clad servitor led us into Regato's study, a high-ceilinged room with enough space for a family of twelve, back home. The fur that covered the couch where we sat wasn't oal. That would have been too easy. It was the pelt of some coal-black animal, glossy and soft.

After the requisite wait—Regato was a busy man, and wanted us to know it—he sauntered in, a tall, slim man with a broad smile creasing his dark face. We stood.

"General Bar-El, it is a pleasure." He clasped Shimon's hand with both of his own. "And this is your aide, Colonel . . .?"

"Hanavi, Senhor."

He smiled vaguely, then dropped into an overstuffed chair, idly smoothing the legs of his suit. "General," he said, "I believe we share a hobby."

Shimon Bar-El didn't return the smile. "I don't have hobbies."

I glared at my uncle, but he ignored it. This was playing along to keep the employer happy? Contradicting the First Senhor of the Assembly didn't seem to quite fit the bill.

Regato's brow furrowed, but he kept his tone light. Perhaps too light. "Oh? I thought we were both devotees of military history." He waved a hand at the bookshelves behind him. "I've studied from Thucydides, to," he said, half-ducking his head, "Bar-El."

Shimon chuckled. "Thank you. But Thucydides was a historian, as you know, not a soldier. And for me, the history of my profession isn't a hobby, it's a matter of business."

"Point welll taken. Your second point, that is. Not your dismissal of Thucydides." Regato raised a finger. "He was, after all, the first to recount battles to preserve them for future generations. I only wish that he had been around later, when Cincinnatus was alive."

"Well, he would have had to live an extra few hundred years. And have been a Roman, instead of a Greek." Shimon Bar-El cocked his head to one side. "Why Cincinnatus?"

Regato touched a button on the table at his elbow. "Coffee, please. Three cups." He raised his head. "Because he reminds me of you, perhaps. If I remember correctly," he said, smiling in self-deprecation, "he, too, was called out of retirement to command an apparently impossible campaign."

A shrug. "Different situation. Cincinnatus was honorably retired. I was cashiered and exiled." He sucked air through his teeth. "Hardly the same thing."

"Hardly a relevant difference on Indess. Even were you capable of taking a bribe, the Cibans would have nothing to offer you. Hunting rights on the oal? You couldn't take advantage of that. Hard currency, the sort Metzada needs? They don't have any. The only offworld trading center is down here."

A servitor arrived with a steaming silver pot of coffee on a tray with three cups and saucers, plus condiments. We were silent until he deposited the tray and left.

Regato himself poured coffee for all of us, then sipped his own and smiled. "Ah. On to business. I received your message, and your instructions were followed to the letter. At a warehouse at the port you will find the rulawood shafts you requested—six thousand of them—and spearheads, boxed separately." He set his cup down on its saucer. "We could have attached them for you."

"Rather have my men do it themselves. You get us all the food I asked for?"

A nod. "All provisions requested. Dried meat and vegetables, enough to feed two thousand for sixty days. If you find you need more of anything, I can have it sent up to you, if you'll provide a guard for the convoy."

"I doubt we will." He shrugged. "I doubt that we'll need sixty days to wrap things up. And we can always cut more rulawood ourselves, if need be. Cibo is heavily forested, so I'm told."

I'd read the report on rulawood, and it sounded useful: similar to bamboo, but lighter and somewhat stronger. It was strong enough that the Ciban villagers had built their walls of it, and were seemingly confident in the walls' strength.

"Good. We also have the wagons and the drayhorses ready." Regato wrinkled his brow, as though he were about to ask why Bar-El wanted the spearshafts ready down here, if he knew there would be plenty of rula where we were going. Or maybe I'm just projecting: that's what I wanted to ask.

"So," he said, steepling his fingers in front of his face, "two questions: first, why didn't you ask to have saddlehorses ready? We could provide them, you know."

"I know. But Metzadans aren't horsemen. And your mounts down here aren't warhorses. I have no intention of putting my men on horseback up against a larger mounted force, every man of whom has grown up as a rider, every one of whom is mounted on a horse that won't panic when some horse or human screams in pain." He shook his head. "We're professionals. Riding warhorses, we'd be amateurs. Riding regular saddlehorses, we'd be doubly amateurs. Not interested."

Regato nodded. "In that case, I understand why you wanted spears you could use as pikes." His thin smile broadened for a moment. "You see, I do know a bit of military history." The smile disappeared. "Second question: how many ninjas do you have with you? I assume you're going to use assassination."

Well, that explained why Regato had been willing to hire us, despite the odds. It wasn't just that he believed in the legend that's grown up around Shimon Bar-El, or Metzada's reputation. He had at least a suspicion, heard a rumor about the Metzadan ninjas.

Shimon Bar-El shook his head. "There aren't such things as ninjas. There haven't been for half a millenium."

He said that with a straight face. Why not? It was true. Metzada's rumored assassins are only referred to as ninjas by offworlders. And they aren't descended from the Nipponese assassins guilds that died out in the nineteenth century.

Not directly descended, in any case. The madmen of the Bushido Brotherhood had been reviving the dying arts.

The cold rock, Metzada, keeps more than one flame burning.

An assassin can be handy to have around in many military campaigns. It can blow an opponent's organization apart if the top general dies; or, better, if he's kept alive, but all his top staff officers and enlisted clerks are killed.

Of course, an assassin has to have some sort of cover, preferably one that will let him mix with the troops, without even his own people knowing what his real job is. Inspector-general is a nice one. You usually get to wear your stars, on your off-hours.

Usually.

Shimon went on: "And it wouldn't do any good, even if we used assassins, which we don't. I doubt a stranger could survive long enough in the main village to find the commander, and then kill him. Even if he did, so what? Villagers, in a situation like this, aren't going to have a top-oriented organization." Bar-El turned to me. "Don't you agree, Colonel?"

He was precisely correct, as usual. Which was why I had no intention whatsoever of killing anyone within the village. Those weren't my orders at all. "Absolutely, General."

Regato spread his hands. "Then how are you going to do it? You're outmanned, in strange territory, and the enemy has greater mobility."

Shimon Bar-El sat back in his chair. He pulled out a tabstick and thumbed it to life, ignoring the one already smoldering in the ashtray, then took a deep drag, exhaling the smoke from his nostrils. For just a moment, the room seemed very, very cold.

"Senhor," he said quietly, "you need access to the mountain."

Regato nodded; his polite veneer faded. "Of course we do—in more ways than one. We need the credits that oal-fur can provide, so that we can bring in power technology, make something of this world. And we need to control the mountains, because the thousand-times-damned Thousand Worlds Commerce Department won't allow reactors on a world that doesn't have a unified government. There are close to a million of us in the valley—we can't allow a few thousand mountain . . . yokels to stand in the way of progress. And let me—"

"Enough." Shimon Bar-El held up a hand. "You're selling a man who doesn't need to be sold. I don't care. I don't care if the Cibans are brave independents defending their homes, or if they're what you say they are. And I don't care whether your motives are pure or corrupt, Senhor; I care that you pay your bills.

"As to how I'm going to do it, I'm not going to talk about that. I don't care to, and I don't have to." He jerked a thumb at me. "I haven't even told my aide how I'm going to do it, what I'm going to do."

I already knew what we were going to do: lose. God forgive me, I knew we were going to lose.

There's an old saying that a battle plan never survives the first contact with the enemy. One of Shimon Bar-El's favorite pastimes was to hold forth on what nonsense that was, pointing at Patton's relief of Bastogne, or Sharon's crossing of the Suez, or Operation Theda Bara, where things went almost exactly as planned—for one side, at least.

"Besides," he'd say, giving the same pause each time, "the last line in the orders, in the plan, should always be the same, should always prevent the plan from becoming obsolete: if all else fails, improvise."

We improvised our way up the slopes of Cibo, the horsemen harassing us all the way. In one sense, it was a standoff: anytime we stopped, the pikemen out in front, protecting the archers behind them, they couldn't do more than taunt us from behind the two-hundred-meter effective range of our bows. And whenever we started to move in the direction of the walled village, they'd sweep down on us, forcing us to form a line, pikemen in the front, and so on.

23

It sounds trivial, and casualties were low on both sides. Two weeks into the campaign, we'd had only three deaths and about twenty-three serious injuries—all skirmishers who had let themselves stray too far from the main body of the force.

Only three. . . . Sometimes I lose my sense of proportion. The three dead meant five or so widows at home, at least a dozen children orphaned.

We were being pushed away from the village, higher up Cibo's shallow slopes. I didn't like it much, as we got nearer the top: all the mountain people had to do was detach a portion of their force, swing around and cut us off at the flat top of Cibo, an extinct volcano.

"Don't bother me with technicalities, Colonel," Bar-El snapped, sitting on the waist-high rock. He beckoned to and then whispered to a runner, who nodded and loped over to where Silverstein's battalion was camped, at the far edge of the clearing. "I'm in no mood to be quibbled with. I don't give a damn whether this pile of rock and dirt is a mountain, a volcano, or a pile of elephant dung."

We'd let the Cibans force us to climb too far—at least in my opinion. Three klicks away, and about one klick below us, the walls of the village peeked mockingly, just barely visible behind the trees. Still, I could get occasional glimpses of people and animals moving in the narrow streets, and a mass of horses and men milling around the main gate.

I swallowed, hard. I'd stalled long enough. The Law doesn't apply when we are away from Metzada, but that doesn't mean that what we have to do doesn't affect us.

"Tetsuo, what is it?" he asked.

I shook my head. "Nothing. Just looks like they're sending out another detachment." The sun hung low in the sky, a white ball that was painful to look at. "Think they're preparing for an assault?"

He bit off a piece of jerky, washing it down with water from his belt canteen. "Unless they figure they need another thousand men to deliver an invitation to tea." He hung the canteen back on his belt, then retrieved a tabstick from his shirt pocket. "Probably they're going to take off tonight—cover of darkness and all that—try and swing around the top of the mountain, cut us off, then come at us from two directions."

The locals' only projectile weapons were crossbows. It was possible to fire them one-handed from horseback, but the rate of fire was pitiful. Reloading a crossbow on horseback was probably not a whole lot easier than firing one from a pitching, yawing saddle.

But from prepared positions, they could sit behind barricades on solid ground and choose their shots. As a matter of fact, it was possible, at least in theory, that one or more of them had already done that and were lying in ambush, somewhere near us.

A handy possibility, that.

Shimon Bar-El rose. "Take a walk with me."

The downslope edge of the clearing was just that: an edge. A hundred meters below, the sharp drop ended in a stand of the ever-present rula trees. Bar-El gestured at the village below. "About how many would you say are in this next group?"

I shrugged. "A thousand or so. Maybe a touch more." We now had almost all of the local effectives after us.

I glanced over my shoulder. There was nobody in the vicinity. It wasn't impossible that Shimon Bar-El would slip over the edge, and maybe drag his aide with him. At least that's what it would look like. There was a convenient overhang, maybe fifty meters down. I could probably climb down and duck under before anyone could reach the edge.

And then I'd hide until dark. It's easy to hide in the dark. You become darkness, and drift through the night.

And then, when Yonni Davis took command, not knowing what Shimon Bar-El had planned, he'd have no choice but to withdraw, and quickly, quickly, before the villagers got their second force of horsemen around the mountaintop, and cut off the line of retreat. Over the mountain and down the other side; the regiment would make it to the port within a week, and leave Indess behind. They would have retreated out of an impossible situation, having relied on a Shimon Bar-El fix that had died with Shimon Bar-El.

Old Rivka had planned it well. We'd collect the credits due us under the contract, and with minimal casualties and little damage to Metzada's reputation. Payment-under-all-contingencies contracts would be harder to come by, but what of that? All-contingencies deals come along once in a lifetime; the loss of revenue wouldn't be much.

In a few weeks, when somebody who only looked vaguely like Tetsuo Hanavi appeared at the lowland port and booked passage out, nobody would suspect a thing. I'd make it home, and tell a story of lying under a pile of leaves with a broken leg.

Easy.

I turned, slowly. Bar-El had pulled out his utility knife, and locked the killing blade into place.

"What's that for?"

He smiled. "I know you're a wizard with the Fairbairn, but are you any good with this?"

I could have sliced him from throat to crotch in less time than it would have taken him to blink. But Bar-El knifed by his aide was not the image I wanted to leave behind. The death that would trigger the retreat was supposed to look like the result of an enemy assassination, or an accident. The image would have to be maintained in front of the line troops; what they didn't know, they couldn't ever tell.

"Reasonable," I said. "I may be just a staff officer, but I try to keep in shape."

"So I recall." He chuckled, backing away from the edge before unlocking the blade and clicking it back into the body of the knife. "What I meant was, how good are you at cutting wood with this thing? I want to gather a bit for the fire tonight. Good exercise."

The runner he'd earlier dispatched joined us, barely panting.

" 'Silverstein to Bar-El: What the hell are you doing, Shimon?' " The runner, a tall, skinny private who looked about seventeen, shrugged an apology before continuing. " 'We're cutting wood, as per orders, and have relayed said directions to other battalions, but I'm damned if I understand what we're trying to do. Would you be good enough to enlighten me?' "

He nodded. "Good. Tell him: we're starting a bonfire tonight, and I'm particular about the length of the firewood. Soon as it's dark—say, in another ninety minutes—leave First Company on watch, and get the hell up the trail to this clearing. Same thing for the Third Battalion. I don't want any interruptions from the locals."

A fire wasn't a bad idea; it could cover a retreat. I smiled at him. "So that was your idea? A bonfire? Do you want me to go into the woods and cut my own contribution?"

He clapped a hand to my shoulder. "Not a bad idea. I think I'll join you." He flexed his fingers. "I can use the exercise. These things are starting to get limber again." A few weeks of treatment from a medician can do wonders for arthritis.

He nodded to the runner, who was still standing there. "That's it. Run along." He turned to me. "Coming?"

I followed him into the woods. Good; he was taking us out of sight of the encampment. Perhaps it wouldn't be as neat a solution for him simply to disappear along with his aide, but it wouldn't take long for David to notice, and if a search didn't find his body, Yonni would have to attribute it to the opposition.

I let my hand slide to the hilt of my Fairbairn. Just another moment, until he was stepping over the tree. He might be Bar-El the Traitor, but he was my uncle, and I loved him. I'd make it as painless as possible.

I drew my knife, and—

Pain blossomed in the back of my head. I tried to lift the knife—*never mind, finish him off, finish it, finish it, you have to finish it*—but it grew heavier, and heavier. Something hissed at me, and then rough hands seized me from behind, dragging me back.

I gave up, and fell into the cool dark.

* * *

I woke to someone slapping me with a wet cloth. There was a shooting pain in my head; with every heartbeat, the little man inside drove another nail into my skull.

I tried to say something, but I'm not sure how it came out.

"Easy, Tetsuo." Yonni Davis's voice was calm as always. "I hit you a bit harder than I should have, but," he said, gentle fingers probing at my scalp, sending more rivulets of pain through my head, "I don't think you've got a concussion."

I opened my eyes, slowly. It was dark—and it took me a moment to realize that some of the lights dancing in my eyes were stars overhead.

Somewhere in the darkness, Shimon Bar-El chuckled. "It's probably my fault. I took the wrong hypo out of the medician's kit. Morphine. Didn't just put you under, Tetsuki, it almost killed you. Yonni, you sure he's going to live?"

"Good chance."

"Let's get him up."

Far away, there was a rustling, as though a ship's sails were flapping in the wind. Sails?

Hands grasped my arms, pulling me to my feet. It was hard to tell, but at the opposite end of the clearing, next to the ledge, it looked like the shelter halves were being . . . thrown off the edge?

I blinked, trying to clear my eyes and head. I was still muzzy from the morphine.

"They're called hang gliders, Tetsuki," Shimon Bar-El said, puffing on a tabstick, then handing it to me. "You take a specially designed piece of cloth—say, one that's been camouflaged as a shelter half—and then you attach it to three spears, one at each leading edge and one down the middle. And then you attach cables and bracing spars, and re-rig the pack harnesses to hold a soldier up instead of a pack down."

He chuckled. "Instant air power. Then you have your men practice for a few hours, taking short flights across the clearing, before you make it real."

I turned. He was rubbing at his chin.

"Frankly," he said, "I doubt that one in ten will actually be able to control the silly things well enough to put their gliders down inside the walls. But the village is vulnerable now— most of the men of fighting age are up here, chasing shadows. Once we get the gates open . . ."

He shrugged, then smiled. "Not as bloody as the Casa wars, eh?"

"You did it."

He actually laughed. "You, my dear nephew, have a keen eye for the obvious." He clapped a hand to my shoulder. "Of course I did it. Come morning, the few effectives inside the city will be captured or dead, and then we can see how much the Ciban horsemen like exchanging bowshots with their wives and children tied to the walkways around the walls. I think we'll be able to persuade them to move on. Lots of other places to settle on on this continent." He looked up at me, quizzically. "You like it?"

"You intended this from the first."

He spat. "Of *course* I did. The only worry was whether we were going to sneak the sails past the Commerce Department. I thought the messkits made a nice distraction, didn't you?" He looked at me long and hard. "Don't underestimate me again, Tetsuo. It wouldn't be safe." He brightened. "I do have a job for you, though. If the local horsemen try being stubborn, it would be kind of handy if they start fighting among themselves. The leader taking a crossbow bolt in the chest might be a nice way to start things."

He grinned. "Get going."

I met him at the port a few weeks later. The regiment was loading itself onto shuttles, preparatory to leaving. Leaders are first down, last up; we had some time to talk.

"Nice bit of work with the crossbow, Tetsuki. Old Yehoshua taught you well."

I shrugged. Moving through the dark is something I do well; the crossbow shot that had taken the Ciban leader in the throat had been a lucky one. "No problem, General."

He started to turn away.

"Uncle?"

He turned back, startled. "Yes?"

"You knew from the beginning, didn't you?"

"Of course, and send my regards to the deputy premier. A nice idea," he said, nodding, "arranging an all-contingencies contract where Metzada gets paid whether or not we win, and then working out a way to lose cheaply, without losing face, sacrificing only an old irritation."

31

He thumped himself on the chest. "An old irritation. I can just see you explaining it to Regato: 'Sorry, Senhor, but the only one who could have successfully generaled such a campaign was Shimon Bar-El—you knew that when you hired us.'" He spread his hands. "'And since the old traitor is dead, we had no choice but to retreat. Now, our contract calls for payment under all contingencies. Do you pay us now, or do we have the Thousand Worlds Commerce Department garnishee all your offworld credits until you do?'"

He lit a tabstick and then chuckled. "That is how it was supposed to go, no?"

"Roughly." I shrugged. "But I think I'd have had a bit more tact, a bit more finesse. Shimon, if you knew all that, why? Why did you—"

"Stick my head in the buzzsaw?" He shrugged his head. "I could tell you that I knew that my hang glider gambit would work, but that'd be a lie. True as far is it goes, but . . . Regato told you about Cincinnatus, Tetsuo. About how he chose to come out of retirement, to command the armies of Rome again. I don't think Regato could have told you why. It wasn't just that he wanted the taste of blood in his mouth again. It was the same for him as for me.

"I was a bad husband, a horrible father, and I've never been a good Jew, Tetsuki. But I am a general. Commanding an army is the one thing I do right." His faint smile broadened. "And I wouldn't have missed this for anything." He stuck out his hand. "Which is why we say goodbye here."

"What do you mean?"

He sighed. "You haven't been listening. Let's say I go back to Metzada with you. Do you think there's any chance Rivka is going to recommend to the premier that I get my stars back?"

No. She'd been clear about that; I wasn't to even offer that to Bar-El as bait. Not because she'd been worried about paying— dead collect little—but because he never would have believed it. Metzada's reputation had been badly hurt by his selling out on Oroga; the damage would be irreparable if we let him come back and return to permanent duty.

He nodded. "Correct. This was a special case. I'll be taking the next civilian shuttle up, and then heading back to Thellonee. New Britain colony, most likely—probably just hang around New Portsmouth. Perhaps another special case will come up someday. If you need me, find me." He turned his back on me and started walking from the landing field.

"Uncle?"

He turned, clearly irritated. "What is it?"

"Did you take that payoff on Oroga?"

Shimon Bar-El smiled. "That would be telling."

PART ONE METZADA

If brothers live together, and one of them dies childless, the wife of the dead brother shall not marry one not of his kin; her husband's brother shall marry her, and perform his duty to her. Her firstborn shall take the name of the dead brother, that his name be not blotted out among Israel.

But if the man refuses to take his brother's wife, then his brother's wife shall go up to the gate, to the elders, and say, "My husband's brother refuses to maintain his brother's name in Israel; he will not perform the obligations of a husband's brother to me."

Then the elders of the city shall call him, and speak to him, and if he persists and says, "I will not take her," then his brother's wife shall come close to him in the presence of the elders, and loose his shoe from his foot, and spit in his face.

And she shall say, "*This* is what is done to the man that does not build up his brother's house."

—Deuteronomy 25:5–9

CHAPTER ONE The Wolf

Each year it gets a little harder to put it all back together. That includes me, as well as everything else.

I was in a reconstructive therapy session when the deputy premier called.

"Again, Tetsuo, again," P'nina Borohov said, pushing down on my right leg as I tried to raise it.

P'nina was one of the ugliest women I've every seen. Well into her forties, she was easily seventy pounds overweight, thick-waisted with muscle, not fat. Pig-faced, mustached—and with fingers like steel clamps.

One of the ways we're taught to deal with pain is by concentrating on something extraneous. She had a mole below her mouth, right on the jawline, with three long, black hairs sticking out of it. I tried to focus my attention on how ugly it was, but that didn't help much.

I hurt.

Everything hurt: a side-effect of one of the drugs they give you when they have to regenerate certain kinds of damage quickly. They call it NoGain. It's expensive as all hell, and it doesn't work with valda oil. Anything more, I don't Need to Know.

Normally, after the aborted kneecapping I'd received in Eire, I could have looked forward to perhaps as much as a couple thousand hours of rest and gradual physical therapy, accompanied by whatever reconstruction and occupational therapy the fourth-best reconstructive surgeon on Metzada prescribed. Except for some of the occupational therapy, which I'd have enjoyed, it would have been a rough regimen, but I'd been through it before.

But this wasn't normal.

The stainless steel therapy table was painfully cold against my back as I lay there, wearing nothing but a thin pair of cotton shorts. The light of the overhead glow hurt my eyes.

My heart thudded slowly in my chest, each dull beat a dismal, distant ache. That's the thing I hate most about NoGain; even when it doesn't put me through agony, it leaves me feeling exactly the way I do when somebody I love dies.

When I was a boy, I thought heartache was just an expression.

Boys can be such fools.

Her fingers hurt.

"Again, Tetsuo," she said, digging a knuckle into the back of my calf. That wasn't for therapy, not directly. It was just to force me to do what she wanted me to.

"You will—"

"You will be telling us what you are doing here," he says.

He is the slightly larger, the fractionally older of a pair of big men in the black uniforms of Irish Republic guardsmen, politely wondering what somebody with no Sein ID is doing on the cobblestones of a Dublin back street. He rubs a large hand against his stubbled chin in curiosity while his partner sticks a spearpoint under

my chin to push me up against the battered brick wall
so they can comfortably inquire.

"Sooner or later," he says. "Sooner or later." He slaps
his nightstick against his palm. It isn't as though he's
threatening me with it. It's more like he's fine-tuning,
either the stick or himself. "Sooner or later, you will be
telling us. I say again— "

"Again. But harder this time. You're not scheduled for more
NoGain sessions; we have to make this last one count."

I pushed up my leg, my knee setting up a scorching, rip-
ping pain that made me think she was going to tear the leg
right off.

The sadist responded by pushing down harder.

There's supposed to be a point at which pain becomes so
great that it overloads the mind; the mind blanks, and the
victim smiles at his torturer. I don't believe in it, and I'm not
sure P'nina did, but she was accelerating toward that point,
like a ramscoop trying for lightspeed, knowing that it will
never make it, but feeling that the effort is enough, will do
enough, will result in—

"Enough!"

"Hardly. Push back."

I screamed.

Granted, I usually wear a soldier's uniform, but I'm a butcher,
not a hero. I'm not downplaying my skills—

Long-practiced skills come into play when the more
soft-hearted of the two Irishmen drops the spearpoint
and lets me collapse to the ground.

I fall hard, limp, to the rough stones. It's a high art to
fall hard without hurting yourself, but it's not art, not
for me, not now. I'm just a man in agony.

But then I move.

Half-blind with pain, I brace myself on my hands, grit
biting hard into my palms, making them bleed, but you
need a tripod. Mine is two palms and a hip. I lash out

with my good leg, steel-toed boot bites hard, deep into the soft muscle of his calf; on the backswing, heel catches him square on the shinbone. I fall to my shoulder while I slip my baby Fairbairn knife out of my left sleeve and into my right hand.

Fingers tighten on the grip; I slash upward into his partner's groin. Slash-twist-pull-and-recover, and his eyes widen first in surprise, then narrow in pain. His high-pitched, womanlike scream makes my ears ring as I pull away my blood-drenched hand, watching him clutch the dark stain spreading across his crotch.

I turn to finish off the soft-hearted guardsman.

His mouth works soundlessly as clumsy fingers try to block my knife.

But he can't do it. I may be a butcher, but—

—I was one of the best in the Section, and I'd been one of the old woman's favorite utility fixers for the better part of five years and two promotions, one of which even shows in the star I wear on each shoulder.

Still, I am definitely the kind of person who has to carry an exit-pill when he's carrying more knowledge in his head than is safe. I know a few iron men, several who can go through unbelievable agony without it showing on their faces. Dov is like that. The Sergeant, sure. Zev, sometimes. Benyamin was, too. I've seen pictures of Benyamin standing next to Dov, and I know that my brother wasn't as much of a giant, but that's not the way I remember him.

Benyamin was a hero.

I'm not. I threw back my head and screamed, until I thought my lungs were on fire.

The thing about physical therapists is that they just don't care. She pushed down, and I pushed back with my leg, until the chorus of agony reached a crescendo that made me think the whole universe was going to split open.

At that moment, the phone on the wall chimed twice, then three times.

"My signal! My signal!" I shrilled, suddenly a child excused from a spanking.

"Ten seconds." With a skill that came from years of practice in handling barely-compliant flesh, P'nina eased me back to the table with one hand and strapped my knee down tightly, while another snatched up a cotton ball and bottle of alcohol from the porcelain-topped stand at her side. She quickly cleaned and sterilized a spot near my knee, dropped the bottle back on the white table, tossed the cotton ball toward the recycler, brought up, readied, and stuck in a needle.

I know it was a sharp needle, expertly applied. But NoGain turned what should have been a brief pinch into an awful stabbing—

—knife rises and falls of its own volition, drinking blood, stabbing down into what had been a face, again and again, all concentration, all skill gone.

Skills come and go, when it's real. In the final analysis, everything fails us.

The knife falls from my hands; I crouch there in the blood and the mud and the shit, and weep.

Reflexively, I clean my knife on a dead man's shirt, then, using the kinder guardsman's spear as a crutch, I pull myself up. Balancing on my good leg, I hobble off into the night, not stopping for a moment to bid the corpses farewell.

Gestures don't belong in Section. We are what we are.

Sometimes, though, I just don't know what I am. Sometimes, it feels like the part of me that was little Tetsuo Hanavi has vanished—

—which quickly vanished, as a warm glow spread from the spot where the needle had gone in.

There are no nerves for pleasure, but I'll tell you what pleasure is: it's when pain goes away in a spreading cloud of warmth.

I basked in the glow as I snapped my fingers and pointed to the phone.

"You can get it yourself in a moment. Be good for you." She unstrapped me, then folded her ample arms over her ample bosom.

I glared once. It's called command presence, and something even an imitation general is expected to be able to produce upon demand.

Surprising both of us, it worked: she uncrossed her arms and tossed me the phone.

"Tetsuo Hanavi," I said, gesturing at P'nina to leave the room. "I'm not alone; wait a moment." If it was important enough to interrupt me in PT, it was something P'nina didn't have the need to know.

She slid the door shut behind her. In the waiting room outside, there were other patients. A lot of us need putting back together; four of them were waiting for their turn in P'nina's gentle hands.

"We're alone," I said, reaching over to the dressing table for my pants and struggling to get my bad leg in first.

"I need something done," the old woman's voice husked in my ear. "Are you fit to travel?"

Since she could have punched up the latest medical report on me—she'd probably just done so—the question wasn't whether or not I was in peak condition, but whether I thought I could travel on a cane and arrogance, at least for the time being.

"Yes." Although I wouldn't require the cane. You learn to give up crutches as soon as you can.

"How soon can you be here?"

I glanced at my thumbnail and then shrugged before remembering that this was voice-only; when I'm home, I sometimes let myself not pay enough attention to what's going on. It's a luxury. "In case you've forgotten, the Twentieth is only an hour or so out. If it can wait until then, let it. I want to meet the first shuttle."

My brother's, Ari's, regiment is the Twentieth.

I once had four brothers. Ari, Shlomo, Kiyoshi, and Benyamin; Ari the baby, Benyamin the oldest.

The line of dead stretches out past my vision. I can only make out a few of the closer faces, sometimes just my brothers'.

I see traces of Kiyoshi's face when I look in the mirror. It's not just that we were similar-looking; it's that the blond blandness of our faces is always belied by our Nipponese first names. I never liked Shlomo. I will always remember Benyamin.

Family Hanavi and clan Bar-El memorialize Shlomo, Kiyoshi, and Benyamin yearly, at the Yarzheit ceremony, along with all the others of the legions of the dead.

I remember them every day.

My brother, Ari. . . .

Fingers clacked on keys in the background. "I'd rather see you now," she decided. "If I send you on this one, your team is leaving in a week, at the outside. You'd be going with Alon to Thellonee. Which doesn't give you long to put a team together."

If? I thought.

"If," she answered. She can't read minds—it just seems that way at times. "Pinhas's trust in you to the contrary, I'm not sure it's right for you. It involves your uncle."

"Your uncle." I had two living uncles. She wasn't talking about the Sergeant.

"We've gotten a note from him," she went on. "Quote: 'Freiheimers are rivetting their tanks. I know something else of use to you. But I am valuable where I am.' End of quote; and end of message. It was smuggled in via an Orogan trader. I'm having the first part researched, but I can already interpret the second part to mean either that he puts a high price on what he knows, or that he wants you to get him out of whatever mess he's into. Or, more likely, both."

Probably both. Since he was exiled, Shimon had found that other armies besides ours could make use of his mind, although he had worked only on a consulting basis, and only in wars where Metzada was not involved.

A very clever man. He knew full well that neither the

government, clan, nor the family would tolerate him bucking Metzada.

Still, the old woman is the second most devious person I know, but maybe she was reading a bit too much into twenty words from the most devious person I know.

"It can wait." Putting together a team, even quickly, wouldn't be a problem. I'd have Zev as my second, and grab whoever in Section was around. Not a nice bunch of people, but niceness is not an important quality in headsmen.

"I'll have Levine here in fifteen minutes," she said, as though that ended the matter.

The old lady's background is Foreign Service, not Section. She's never really understood that chain-of-command doesn't really work when you're usually on your own. The kind of independence of action you get used to in the field tends to stick when you're home.

Sometimes it tends to push you too far out on a tangent, makes you act too independently. I once had a partner who did that. Once.

In any case, I wanted to see my brother. It was one thing to read the flash that said he was still alive, that his injuries were minor; it's another to touch, flesh to flesh.

"I'll see you after the shuttle touches down," I said, then set the phone down when she didn't answer.

Better finish getting dressed.

I limped over to the side of the wall for my shoes, and then stooped to pick up the khaki shirt with the star on each epaulet.

There were far too few campaign ribbons above the left pocket for such hardware on the shoulders. One thing about being inspector-general is that you are, officially, a noncombatant, and noncombatants don't earn campaign ribbons. The four ribbons are reminders of the days when I was a real soldier. The time when I was pretending to be something I wasn't, instead of pretending not to be what I am.

Whatever that is. A shochet, minus the ritual, at best.

I shrugged into the shirt and buttoned it before picking up

my cane and heading for the door. I hung the cane on a hook by the door.

Eventually, you have to give up crutches, of all kinds.

Out in the waiting room, at the end of the row of four patients waiting for their turn with P'nina, Zev Aroni sat, waiting patiently, a briefcase on his lap, going through some paperwork. We have to actually do some IG things, to keep up appearances.

"I'm done, Sergeant," I said. "Let's go."

Zev's dark face was expressionless, as usual. Wordless, he accompanied me into the corridor as I limped toward the nearest tube entrance. Sergeant Zev Aroni was officially my aide—but as with most things in Section, appearances are true, but only part of the truth; Zev was my partner. Junior partner, usually. Not always.

I never really liked Zev, which wasn't a problem. You're not supposed to like your partner. I mentioned that once, to a new Section draftee I was training. He asked why. "Because it doesn't hurt so much when you have to shoot him for going lame on you," I said. He thought that was a figure of speech, until the first time he went offplanet on a Section assignment— and one cold, wet night in a forest in Thuringia, broke his leg.

"I heard your signal," Zev finally said, when there was nobody around to overhear us. "Rivka?"

"She wants to see me. Us." I nodded. "But we're going to meet Ari, first."

He frowned at that. "Not a good idea to buck the deputy, Tetsuo."

"You want to do something about it?"

"Not me." He smiled, a gap-toothed whiteness that seemed overly bright in a face the color of bitter coffee that's been lightened with only a hint of milk. "Not me. I'm your *partner*."

"Right."

Zev at my side, I limped my way out into the corridor and the warrens, toward the tube.

CHAPTER
TWO The Bear and the Lion

There aren't any real surprises when the first troop skipshuttle lands on Metzada. It lands; it's taxied to the elevator; it's lowered into Metzada; a group of men, some of them short a few pieces, all of them bone-tired, get off.

Simple.

Straightforward.

We've been in contact since the transport cleared the Gate, and appropriate notices have already been distributed to clan and family of the dead and wounded; widows and orphans are entitled to know, as soon as is possible, that they are widows and orphans. Clan elders have been alerted to station seniors near tube entrances to turn back family members whose understandable want to see wounded loved ones would, if acted upon, interfere with what has to be done.

At least, there aren't supposed to be surprises—even minor ones.

Emptying an orbiting troop transport is primarily a problem in logistics. When I was a boy I was fascinated by logistics, and thought I might like to specialize in it. The science and art of matching materiel to needs has always enchanted me. I was tapped—too early, in my opinion—for Section, and I never had the chance to study it formally, but the fascination remains, and maybe some of the orientation.

My uncle Shimon, for example, has always talked of Patton's Third Army's relief of Bastogne as the greatest cavalry maneuver of all times. He's right, of course, but to me, it's the most beautiful logistics exercise in history. The trick wasn't just pulling an army out of a winter battle, turning it ninety degrees, and marching it a hundred-fifty kilometers to launch an attack, it was to make sure that when Patton's troops started the attack, enough supplies would arrive that they could finish it. A gorgeous exercise. . . .

The problem of landing a regiment starts skyside. Let me give you the numbers: the ships the Thousand Worlds uses as troop transports each have only two shuttlebays, one port, one starboard. A skipshuttle can hold only a few more than five hundred men—fewer if there are wounded among them. If we're lucky, there's about two thousand Metzadans in the troop transport.

Two trips per ship, right? Two waves, two orbits, yes?

No. Remember, we still have to get a skipshuttle back up to the transport for the third and fourth wave, and, practically speaking, only one skipshuttle can leave or depart per orbit. Now, if we didn't have to reuse the specific skipshuttles that came with the transport, it'd be easier. But TW pilots fly the shuttles, and each of them will fly only his own ship. Which means that even after his ship touches down and we unload it, we still have to boost it back up to the surface, haul it five klicks down the runway to the TW laser launcher, and let them refit it for launching.

Minimum turnaround time on a skipshuttle is about eight hours; the ablative launch engines are basically just popped in after the casing and ashes of the previous engine are cleaned out; filling the maneuvering tanks, testing and—if necessary—blackboxing avionics packages takes a while.

But there's no operational bottleneck there; that's all as fixed as the movements of the planets in the sky. The only bottleneck we can do something about is down here.

Medical has long been alerted: operating rooms are heated up to handle priority cases; surgeons and assistants have been put through a forced-sleep regimen and wakened just early enough so that they'll be over their early-morning drowsiness when the skipshuttle touches down. Emergency-medicine specialists, both physicians and medicians, are hustled to the port, medics stripped from homebound regiments and slotted into support companies to give the doctors what help they need.

The transport orbiting above has to be cleared quickly, and in the appropriate order: the wounded first, followed by the unwounded troops, and finally the officers and the commander. Officers—except for wounded, of course—are first-down-last-up offworld; returning to Metzada, they're first-up-last-down.

Everybody has a place around the huge combination elevator/airlock that lowers the skipshuttle down into Metzada—you're "on" Metzada when the wheels touch down on the frigid runway; you're "in" Metzada when you're underground, where we live. There are eighteen airtight doors circling the bottom of the shaft; no matter how the skipshuttle is positioned, the rear engines are going to block at least three of them, four if it's not positioned quite right on the elevator.

But that still leaves at least fourteen usable doors. Even if you assume it's going to take as much as five seconds apiece to clear a wounded man through a door—it won't, not if the litter carriers are moving—you'd think we could empty a five-hundred man skipshuttle in less than six minutes.

The bottleneck is higher up: the TW skipshuttles only have two exit doors, and the trick is to move in and move the wounded quickly through those. We're lucky if we can empty a skipshuttle in half an hour.

Everybody is there waiting as pumps whir and whine to first purge the lock of as much of the outer air as possible, and then hiss as it adds real, breathable air.

The doctors call what they do triage, but it isn't.

Combat men know what triage is; women don't.

Triage is where you shunt aside those who don't need help because they're not badly hurt—they get treated later—set aside those who are already dead but don't know it—they get buried later—and give priority treatment to those you might be able to save.

Everything to save a life, sure; nothing but the minimum maintenance possible gets done offplant. Reconstruction is saved for the experts, for the women. For one thing, all medics and medicians are, obviously, men—and they're trained to leave what they can to the real doctors.

Like the fourth-best reconstructive surgeon on Metzada: my second wife—who, by the way, has a subspecialty in emergency medicine. Overachievement runs in the family.

Suki didn't notice me as the tube doors wheezed open and I walked into the hallway around lock twelve.

A fat, balding senior sergeant with a logistics pin on his collar walked over to me. He shook hands with me, then with Zev.

"Sofaer," he said, introducing himself. We tend to be rigorous in our informality on Metzada.

"Yes, Sergeant. How goes it?"

"We have a . . . minor problem here."

"Anything I can help with?"

He shrugged. "Perhaps."

"Skipshuttle on runway," speakers blared. *"ETA five minutes."* The team of twenty khaki-clad medics, three white-suited nurses, and two doctors lolled near their airlock, continuing their quiet conversations, as though they hadn't heard. Two medicians played a quiet game of gin over in the corner, while a doctor and her medic assistant involved themselves in some heated but quiet discussion. Everything and everyone was ready to move; there was no need to stand at attention while waiting.

"An unloading problem," Sofaer said. "One of the high-priorities wants to offload last. A bit of laxity in discipline, it seems—in the Third Battalion?" He glanced at me, curious.

So was I. Bad discipline doesn't run in my brother's battalion, although it sometimes seems that way to outsiders. He carries traditional Metzadan informality farther than traditional, although not much farther.

Suki glanced once again through the clear plexi, as though to reassure herself that, indeed, the speakers were telling the truth and the skipshuttle wasn't yet at the bottom of the elevator shaft. She brought her hand up to her throat and whispered into the microphone, then waited for a moment, listening to the voice over her headphones before nodding and yessing.

She was playing with her bun, pretending to tuck a loose strand of black hair back where it belonged, back under the headphone strap, when she first saw me. Momentarily, annoyance swept across her face.

"Business," I said, dismissing the unvoiced objection with a word. She wouldn't want me joggling her elbow any more than I'd want her joggling mine.

She nodded. On Metzada, business trumps everything.

I don't want to describe her. A man's description of his favorite wife has always seemed to me to necessarily either traffic on matters that are properly private—or be manifestly superficial. Let's just say that she's a slim but lovely woman, whose body shows little evidence of having borne three children—two of them by Shlomo, one by me—and whose long black hair is always bound up in public.

Little enough of my life is private. Her waist-length hair enfolding the three of us is something I'll set off, sequester from the rest of my life, shared only with Rachel. It was something I had always envied my brother. Yes, I had lusted after my brother's wife, and when he died, I married her.

The second is common on Metzada; the first was wrong.

When I meet God, I'm going to ask Him why. Not that it'll be my first question.

"ETA four minutes."

Zev, Sofaer and I huddled around her while she spoke into her microphone.

"No," she said to the distant listener. "You tell him that he is to come out when he's assigned to, just like—he won't—? Then have Ari tell him. Dammit, you know that he doesn't take to regeneration—I've got him projected for the OR with the rest of the criticals, and that means he goes right in. No, I've got a schedule to meet, too—there's a brand new right supra-orbital ridge sitting in the mold waiting for . . . never mind. Just tell him to get out in the prescribed order."

She looked over at me. I raised an eyebrow.

"Dov," she said, putting her hand over her microphone. "He says he's coming out with Ari."

Zev smiled. "Dov. Figures."

"That it does." I nodded. "I'll handle it, Sergeant."

Sofaer ingratiated himself to me by accepting that with a nod, walking away, and jacking in his own headset a few meters away.

There are thousands of Dovs on Metzada. But when somebody in the family uses the name without a modifier, it means Master Private Dov Ginsberg.

"What kind of injury?" I didn't see what the problem was. If Dov were awake enough to discuss the matter, his injuries were at least ten days old. Another few minutes could hardly make a whole lot of difference. If he were under treatment, the treatment could be expanded to include an appropriate sedative.

The women in my life seem to read my mind; it annoys the hell out of me. "Not an injury," she said. "And I don't want him already doped up when the anesthesiologist gets her hands on him." She shook her head. "It was shipboard—he's got a hot appendix. Lahav has been pumping him full of valda oil and antibiotics, packing his belly with ice, and sitting up with him for the past week. He should have cut. It's a hell of a lot easier than a godamn bowel resection, which the medicians do all the damn time, but you goddamn men don't have any self-confidence with a knife, unless you're using it to . . . Can you help?"

"Let's see." I pulled my own headset off my belt, plugging it in next to hers as I set it on my head. "Inspector-General Tetsuo Hanavi," I said. "Give me Ari."

"*ETA three minutes. Shuttle on elevator.*" The stone walls vibrated with the sound of distant machinery.

He must have been in the same compartment as the senior medic; it was only a half-second until I heard my baby brother's firm baritone. "Yes, Tetsuo?"

"What the fuck is going on?" I asked, politely.

Zev snickered. He and Ari did not get along. Some people in Section develop a bit of scorn toward those who bear weapons openly, who don't have to pretend.

"Nothing I can't handle," Ari said. "Dov's right here with me. He can hold out another few minutes—he figures he's responsible for me until we're in Metzada."

My uncle Shimon told Dov to watch out for Ari. Dov tends to interpret instructions his own way. Or, rather, the way he thinks Shimon would want him to.

Great. Just what I need, I thought, to get caught in a disagreement between my brother and my wife. Or, more properly, it was Inspector-General Tetsuo Hanavi being caught in a dispute between Lieutenant Colonel Ari Hanavi and Dr. Tetsuko Hanavi.

Ninety-nine percent of me being inspector-general is a fraud; my number-one deputy, a master colonel, is really the IG; I wear the stars both as a cover for my real profession and to keep busies out of Zachariah's hair. Trouble was, this fell into the one percent that isn't.

Usually a problem. Not this time. "Put him on," I said, as I turned my face toward the wall. A whisper is as good as a shout, sometimes.

"One second, then."

"*ETA two minutes.*"

"Yes, sir." It was Dov's voice, flat, emotionless. Real emotion was a part of him that got chopped off long before I ever met him.

"I may be leaving to pay a call on Uncle Shimon shortly." I whispered. "Perhaps within a week. If you have medical clearance, I'll put in for you to go with me. No promises, but I'll put in for it. If you have medical clearance."

There was no answer.

"Dr. Hanavi is your doctor. She will provide medical clearance, if anyone does."

Still no answer.

"You're going to have to spell it out," Zev said. "He's not too bright, our Dov."

I put my hand over the mouthpiece. "Shut up, Zev.—Dov," I went on, taking my hand away, "she won't provide medical clearance if she's angry with you. And I'll have to go see Shimon alone. For whatever purpose I'm assigned."

That registered. "Understood, sir. I will leave the shuttle with the wounded, sir."

I unplugged the phones. "We're all set," I said as I turned to Suki, and went personal long enough for a quick kiss on the lips. "And with—"

"*ETA one minute.*"

"—one minute to spare."

We pay for the life of our people with pieces of ourselves.

Sometimes that's a figure of speech; often it's literal. The teams of stretcher-bearers first brought down men who were missing pieces.

It was a bloodless affair. Outward bleeding had been stopped for hundreds of hours.

"I'll wait here while you have your little reunion." Zev snickered again.

"Just what I was going to suggest." Asshole.

As the stream of stretcher-bearers worked its way from the shuttle toward the doors, I ducked my head as I stepped out into the frosty air, then dodged to one side to avoid two thickset medicians carrying the upper two-thirds of a man on a stretcher. He was missing from about the thighs down.

Don't talk about regeneration therapy. It doesn't always work, and when it does, it takes a bitch of a long time to regrow anything that's both major and peripheral, like a pair of legs. Two years, minimum, until you'll see baby-pink toenails; another year until new muscles learn to work hard enough to match the ones they've replaced. And that's if you push hard on your therapy sessions.

The stretcher cases ended, followed by the walking wounded.

The next man, walking quickly, not at all supported by the medician at his right, seemed unhurt, save that his hands were missing.

The next one, an uninjured man supporting each arm, half-guiding, half-carrying him, had a well-bandaged face, his features swathed in cloth like a mummy. Eyes aren't too bad. Unless the nerves leading back to the brain have been thoroughly damaged, it only takes about six months to grow them back, six months of walking around in the dark.

The next was Master Private Dov Ginsberg.

Dov was a huge and ugly man; his ragged hairline came to within a couple of centimeters of his heavy brows. From within deep sockets, two seemingly unblinking eyes stared coldly at the world as he walked down the stairway from the skipshuttle all by himself, one thick hand pressed against his abdomen, as though trying to hold himself together.

He brought his free hand up against the side of his face, a sound like a butcher slapping a side of beef, then walked out of the line of walking wounded, gesturing me to accompany him.

It's not his size that makes Dov what he is, although that and his strength helps. I'm not sure what it is, really; it's Something Extra. A Talent, Rachel calls it, like the way her mother can work miracles with a cube of rock and a chisel.

It's not his training in hand-to-hand—he's never had any. Master Private Dov Ginsberg is something else. Leave it at that.

"You say you are going to see Shimon." The voice didn't quite match the body. It's almost high-pitched, not at all the basso rumble you'd expect, and it cracks at unexpected moments. That's about the only thing that does. Dov's loyalty to Shimon Bar-El never wavered. It's a personal matter, going back to before his name was either Dov, or Ginsberg—before he was a Metzadan or a Jew.

"I said perhaps." I shrugged. "The old woman got a letter from him. He says he has some knowledge Metzada wants. If it's important enough to involve us, it may—*may*—be important enough to bring you in on." I didn't go into detail.

He thought that over for a moment. "You won't try to hurt him this time, sir." It wasn't really a question. Or a threat. Just random movements of his mouth, while he tried to figure out what Shimon would want him to do.

"Don't be silly," I said. "Of course not." Unless it was necessary. Which he knew as well as I did. He also knew that I'm an inveterate liar. That comes with the job.

But Dov had learned long before that he couldn't kill everyone in the universe who might want to hurt Shimon Bar-El. "I will see you before you leave, sir," he said. "Whether it's with me or without me."

"Very well."

Wordless, he limped off, pressing his hand to his side. At the door, the medicians with Suki hustled him into a wheelchair and rolled him out of sight.

The stream of wounded ended, to be replaced by the rest of the shuttle's human cargo.

I nodded. In the back of my head I'd been keeping a running—or is that limping?—count of the wounded.

Everything can be reduced to numbers. We see six men screaming in pain, lying on the ground, or lying white-faced, eyes distant and unfocused, too far gone to cry. Next to them, we see one man lying dead, and we turn that into a statistic: Metzadan casualties run about five or six injuries to one death. I'd counted two hundred and twelve injured men coming off the shuttle; deaths would run thirty-five and a third, statistically speaking.

There's something special in the face of a soldier getting off a troop carrier; it's the kind of relief you can see in combat when the shot hits the next man.

I made it home, it says. *As I always knew I would.*

The survivor guilt hits later.

The stream of khaki-clad men thinned, then ended, and there was a still moment before he appeared in the door, looking good, but haggard.

My baby brother. Ari Hanavi. When we played as boys, all of us called him the General, even then. We always knew Ari was going to wear stars someday, if he lived. Real stars, not the phony ones the inspector-general wears.

When I was a boy, the generals I saw and heard about—except for Uncle Shimon—were all stern, strong-jawed types. The sort of man who you just *know* could have been a master private if he had only decided to refuse promotion. I've since learned that that's not always true. One of the best generals I've ever met looks more like a shopkeeper than a soldier. Uncle Shimon always looks like an unmade bed.

But my brother fits the stereotype, at least on the outside. And he carried the double oak leaves of a lieutenant colonel on his shoulder like they were a pair of stars.

He paused a moment in the hatch, spotted me, then bounded down the stairs two at a time, apparently not having to readjust himself to Metzada's 120 percent of the standard gravity the transports keep. His knapsack was on his back, and the ancient IMI Desert Eagle he always uses as a sidearm—he may as well carry a handgun; he's a lousy shot, anyway—was in a snapped-down holster at his hip. His hand strayed to tighten his web gunbelt; Ari may have been ready for the heavy gee of home, but his gunbelt wasn't.

Ari always makes a fetish of carrying his own gear. I think that's a rebellion against Uncle Shimon, who always went into battle carrying nothing more than a notepad and a few spare stylos. There's something to be said for doing it your own way, no matter what that way is.

Behind him, loaders closed the skipshuttle's hatches and pulled the rolling stairways away, shooing all of us toward the doors.

He extended his hand as we walked toward the nearest door. His handshake was firm and warm. The only injury that I could see was on his left hand, and that covered by a clean bandage.

He dismissed my look of concern with a quick pursing of his lips.

"I see you made it," I said.

He shook his head, dismissing that. "Problem." He was still in general-officer mode. "We had some men captured by the Legion. They caught a platoon assault group during a sweep."

"And?"

"Some legionnaires decided to make Haim Elazar talk. They cut off his hands."

I nodded. About the only other way a man can lose both of his hands without getting killed is in bomb-disposal work.

"They hacked them off," Ari said. "For practice. For fun."

"What happened to the platoon?"

He smiled. "A very pretty diversion and rescue. We got all the live ones out. 'The Legion may be tough—' "

" '—but they're still dumb.' "

The French Foreign Legion is still, after all these centuries, an army of moderately well-trained scum soldiers, but they're scum soldiers under tight discipline, always commanded by Saint Cyr officers, although the Legion's home is now on Thellonee, rather than Corsica, for obvious reasons: it's a hell of a lot easier to recruit scum on Thellonee than anywhere else.

Neither Metzada nor the Legion would like to get into a private war, which would serve neither the interests of Greater France nor of Metzada—so we tend to tiptoe around each other. They do more tiptoeing, and that's the way we like it. Rule of thumb: Metzadan line troops can, all things being equal, beat Legion scum soldiers about eighty percent of the time, but the only general to do so without taking horrible casualties has been Shimon Bar-El.

Our casualties are the only ones that count. Casualties among legionnaires don't matter to the French; that's the advantage of using scum soldiers. They're usually people you'd have to jail or shoot anyway.

As we stepped through the door, two gray-suited loaders slammed it shut and then spun-locked it.

There were easily forty soldiers crowding the lock, waiting for Ari, rather than rushing off to their families. That's one of the perks of being a line officer: you get the chance to earn some loyalty. People do things for you that they don't have to.

A tired-faced private who looked, and probably was, about seventeen, spoke up. "What's happening about Haim, Ari?" He called my brother by his first name, but he made it sound like he was saying "sir."

Ari raised his voice. "Everybody, *go home*. I've put in the complaint." He looked over at me. "You'll get the official charge later. For now?"

"I'll get busy on it, as soon as I see the deputy premier. Which will be any time now. But I'll still need the paperwork."

"You'll have it. I'll do it tonight."

"*Sure* you will, Ari." Zev snorted. Sometimes Zev didn't have the brains God gave Frenchmen.

Two sergeants and three privates started to turn toward him, desisting when Ari gave a quick shake of his head.

"Families," he repeated. "Go."

The question would be how to deal with it, and that would be at least partly political. We had long had an explicit POW agreement with the Legion commandant; my quasi-deputy had negotiated it himself, back before I became IG. Basically, full Geneva rights adhere to prisoners properly belonging to the Legion and Metzada—and each command was responsible for punishing any lapses of its own people, and denying tactical advantage to any unit where infractions occur.

A medician pushed his way through the crowd, a phone in

his hands. He jacked the base into the wall. "The deputy wants to see you now, she says."

Ari raised his eyebrows. "Something hot?"

"Family matter," I said, as I decided to take Rivka's "you" to mean all three of us. I held out my hand for the phone; the medician handed it to me.

I opened the phone, said, "On our way," listened for a second, heard nothing, snapped it shut, and handed it back.

CHAPTER THREE "Make It Look Like an Accident"

Metzada, Bar-El Warrens
Effron family quarters
12/20/43, 1348 local time

I've always thought that we live too close to our archetypes.

It's rare that we get a general who doesn't think of himself as Ariel Sharon, Mickey Marcus or David Warcinsky, unless he thinks of himself as another King David. Too many privates think of themselves as Samson in the Temple. Colonels in assault battalions tend to think they're Yonatan Netanyahu. I never met a male politician who didn't think he was really Moses, going to lead us back to Earth, back home to Eretz Yisrael. I doubt there's a female politician who doesn't, in her heart of hearts, think of herself as Golda Meir.

Except for the age and the hair, Deputy Premier Rivka Effron didn't look the part. She was a short, slim woman, who looked about sixty, and had looked about sixty for the past ten years. Her gray hair was tied in a tight bun, only a few strands out of place. She tried to pat them back into place as she ushered us out of the public corridor and into her quarters.

"You're late," she said to me, softening the words with a

smile that she didn't mean. "We were going to start without you. Welcome back, Ari," she said.

She didn't mean it. She meant, *What are you doing here?*

"Thank you, Aunt Rivka," he said, as though he meant it. Which he didn't.

Just to be sociable, I would have said something I didn't mean, but I couldn't think of anything really good.

"Aunt Rivka," I said. That was close enough. She wasn't really our aunt, but my mother's sister's aunt—call that whatever relationship you want to. Well, actually, Aunt Leah is really what people on other worlds would call my mother's half-sister, although we don't use the "half" designation in Metzada. Those who are blood of my blood and bone of my bone are not half of anything.

Modest living is part of the Golda image; except for the walk-in kitchen on one end and the private shower and toilet on the other, the apartment was a typical one-room, suitable for up to three adult bachelors or a single or paired widow with no children at home: basically, a single, a box four meters square, two and a half meters high. Inside was a couch that could convert into a bed at night, a table, and a dozen chairs stacked in the corner for visitors. In the far corner of the room, a desk with a terminal stood next to the delivery tube. The rug was a simple surface-grass mat.

An old copy of a Chagall print decorated the far wall; on the stone coffee table there was a bust of Rivka's second husband Yaacov that, even to my untrained eye, was clearly the work of Rachel's mother.

Two of the chairs had been unstacked, and both were occupied: one by tall, ganging Pinhas Levine, chief of Section—my boss—the other by Senior General David Alon, who was the new DCSOPS, Deputy Chief of Staff, Operations.

Zev gave me a sideways glance as though to say that he didn't think there was any coincidence in that. Nor any danger, really; everyone in the room was among the small number who knew what I really do for a living.

"Tetsuo, Zev, Ari," Levine said, pronouncing our names like

ticks on a drumhead. He settled his glasses forward on his nose and picked up a sheaf of flimsies.

Alon didn't say anything; he just set down his coffee cup and sat back in his chair, running stubby fingers through thinning hair before folding his hands over his barely-bulging belly. At fifty or so, he was losing both the minor battle of the receding hairline and the more significant campaign against the slide of his chest down toward his waistline, but the war was by no means over.

Zev unstacked a chair and handed it across the table to me; I set it down for Ari and took the next one for myself.

Rivka gestured us to sit while she went into the kitchenette, coming out with a fresh thermos-pot of coffee and a stack of rolls. "Please. Just out of the oven."

And into the recycler, if there's a God.

I repressed a shudder as I poured myself a cup of the weak coffee—on Metzada, luxury items tend not to be very luxurious—and picked up one of the rolls, biting tentatively, while Zev and Ari did the same.

It tasted horrible. Too little salt, too lumpy, and the bottom of it was burnt.

A logical necessity, really; ever since the days of David Warcinsky and the exile to Metzada, we've taken our meals in communal dining halls. Cooking is a profession: it takes a long time to learn how to do it well. Ancient traditions to the contrary, not every woman can cook well, any more than every man can be a great warrior. It's necessary for us, all too often, to force men beyond their abilities in the field; women in the kitchen are a different matter.

"So," she said, taking her seat between Levine and Alon, folding her hands primly in her lap. "Where do we stand?"

Ari looked puzzled. "I haven't put in the paper—"

"The Legion? It's not that. Forget about that." Alon drummed his fingers against his thigh. "It's not that. It's your uncle Shimon."

Levine tapped a flimsy. " 'Freiheimers,' he says, 'are rivetting their tanks. I know something else of use to you. But I am valuable where I am.' Through no coincidence, I'm sure, emissaries of both Freiheim and Casalingpaesa are offering for Metzada's services. We've meetings scheduled with both for just about a thousand hours from now, at the Thousand Worlds preserve on Thellonee."

He indicated Alon with a jerk of his chin. "David's leading a negotiating team. Tetsuo, we want you to go in under cover of it and talk to Shimon."

His face was grim. On matters of business, my boss's face is always grim. One of the things I like about him is that he never bullshits me, never tells me that I've got an easy one.

"It's not all bad." DCSOPS Alon grinned. "Both sides are so jittery they're each paying for travel and the rooms—so we make a profit, even if we turn both down. Which we won't; Freiheim will make an acceptable offer for a regiment to act as cadre, if nothing else. Going to be a deal."

Ari opened his mouth, and then closed it. I knew how he felt.

Ari earned his captain's bars on Neuva Terra under Shimon, fighting for the Casas, fighting the Freiheimers. Ari spent a lot of that time leading Casas; in fact, his first Metzadan command came later, on another world.

But it's credits that keep Metzada spinning. If the money was right, we'd sign on with Freiheim.

That's something even young light colonels ought to understand; it is something people with stars on their shoulders *must*. Metzada is a fragile operation, all too often; we need the offworld credits and the goods that they bring, and Freiheimer money is just as good as Casalingpaesan. Better, when there's more of it.

Levine smiled. "It seems that Shimon feels the same way you do. Does that suggest anything to any of you?"

Ari and Zev shook their heads.

"Nothing," I said, "except that it's important. And not obvious. And that he's in some kind of trouble or he wouldn't have been so cryptic. He wants us to bust him out of whatever mess he's gotten himself into." My uncle wouldn't have arranged a courier-carried message if it weren't important; he wouldn't have put it in the clear if its use were manifest.

"All true." Levine pursed his lips. "The first part didn't suggest anything to me, until I ran it by a couple of Armor boffins."

"Good men," Alon said. "They're working on the new Maccabee XI—"

"David," Levine said, stopping him. Technically, head of Section and DCSOPS are independent, and equals, but Levine reported daily to the premier; even the chief of staff sees the premier only weekly.

"Sorry."

Levine pushed his glasses back. "It seems that the old NAF Army—"

"United States Army," Alon put in. "Pre-NAF. Pre-unification."

"Quite. Well, it seems that for a while, on one model of tank, they used riveted hulls."

"World War II. M3 tanks."

"Trying to save time and money welding a few points." Lev quirked a smile. "Apparently they also saved the time and money a good test would have cost."

"Typical peacetime innovation that shakes right out in combat. It worked just fine," Alon said, "until the tank got hit. Even with a non-killing hit, often some rivets would break loose and rattle around inside."

I shrugged. So what?

Rivka Effron completed the thought. "They rattled around the insides of the tank at bullet speeds, rattling right through the tank crews."

Levine eyed me and Zev levelly. We were expected to see the potentials there, in both directions.

Ari didn't; his eyes went wide. "Which means that a Casa armored cav strike would go through German armor like—"

"Freiheimer," Levine corrected patiently. "They are Freiheimers, not Germans."

Knowing Levine, I read it as a serious reproof, but Ari either didn't see that or didn't care. He just sat back in his chair, clearly satisfied, as though all that that meant was that we now had an edge for hiring on with Casalingpaesa, only pretending to deal with the Freiheimers in order to drive up the price, but . . .

As usual, he was missing the point.

It didn't just cut toward signing on with Casalingpaesa; it also meant that there was some profit to be made by selling a small bit of historical data to Freiheim. Consulting work can sometimes pay well, and you don't get your young men blown to bloody little gobbets when all you're selling is knowledge. Well, most of the time you don't.

Zev spoke up. "So. Do we keep it or sell it? And to which side?"

Ari laughed. It was a full, deep-throated roar, not the hollow laugh that I have.

" 'To which side?' You stupid shit," he said.

Zev's expression didn't change, but a vein in his temple pulsed hard; the room suddenly grew colder. My partner had a wicked temper, and my brother has always had a big mouth.

"Zev." Levine eyed him coldly, his hands resting motionless in his lap. Zev looked at him, then back at me, then shrugged microscopically.

Rivka had missed the whole byplay. "Go on, Ari."

He looked from face to face, at all of us. "You all have been thinking the same thing? You think there's a chance that *Shimon Bar-El* would ever give you something you're going to end up selling to Germans?"

"*Freiheimers*," Alon said, less patience in his voice.

"David." Rivka Effron held up a skeletal hand. "Please. Go on, Colonel."

Dig your own grave.

"To you, perhaps they're *Freiheimers*. But to Shimon, they're Germans. To him, they're *Amalek*." He turned to Zev. "Tell me: how would you feel about going up against, say, Amharic?"

Zev shrugged. His ancestry was largely Beta Yisrael, which accounted for his cafe-just-barely-au-lait skin. The Amharic had ill-treated his ancestors, called them Falasha, enslaved them, murdered them. My ancestors, too, for that matter, although there are no predominantly Beta Yisrael families in clan Bar-El, just adoptees.

"I find it *difficult*," he said, pursed mouth and sardonic tone making it apparent that he also found it *boring*, "to get excited about what somebody did yesterday, much less about what their grandparents did centuries back. Besides," he said as his smile reappeared, "if my ancestors hadn't taken a right when they should have gone straight, they wouldn't have ended up in Ethiopia. The past is dead."

"The past is dead," Alon agreed with a nod. "I'm going to try and get a deal on a whole division, and I don't care which side. If it's Freiheim, though, we're going to have to get something ahead of time for the Bar-El information so they can have their tanks retrofitted."

Ari turned to him. "You never served with my uncle, did you?"

"Not really." Alon shook his head. "We had companies at the same time under Cohen, but we were in different battalions."

"I know you didn't serve under him, or you'd know the verses." Ari's eyes went vague for a moment. " 'Write this for a memorial in the book, and re*hearse* it in the ears of Joshua, for I will *utterly* blot out the remembrance of Amalek from under heaven.' Not my emphasis; his. Or, 'I—I, Shimon Bar-El— remember what Amalek did to Israel, how he *set* himself against him in the way when he came up out of Egypt. Now go and *smite* Amalek, and utterly destroy all that they have, and *spare them not—*' Remember, Tetsuo? Remember?"

I nodded, and shivered, remembering. It's one thing to hear the words in a typical one-room apartment, suitable for up to three adult bachelors or a single or paired widow with no children at home.

It's rather another to sit in a circle about a bonfire, the night before a battle, and watch a quiet prc-battle briefing of what had been a battered regiment, a plea for just one more push before we went home, turn into an exhortation that changed what had been fifteen hundred weary, battered men into fifteen hundred killers with ice in their blood, fire in their nerves, and death in their hands.

Don't tell me it doesn't stand to reason. I was there.

Ari threw up his hands. "Do I look to you like a religious?" he asked, fingers twirling at where earlocks would be. "Do you see payess here?"

Levine's face darkened; he was brought up religious. I was just as happy Ari didn't go on quoting: Levine would have come back with some Mishnah or Gemarah argument about how, in the context of Purim and the identification of Haman as an Amalekite—not to mention Deuteronomy 24:16—being Amalek was a matter of choice, not of ancestry. But that would have moved Ari as little as it would have Shimon, or me—for different reasons, in all three cases.

"I learned from Shimon, on Nueva," Ari said. "It wasn't just business there, not ever. It wasn't Metzada versus Freiheim—it was the Children of Israel versus Amalek. Tetsuo?"

Again, I nodded. I was there, and it was so. "You can talk about Shimon's Children's Crusade as an exception, but it really wasn't. Ask Dov. Unless Shimon's softening in his old age—which I don't believe for a moment—we can go ahead, explore it, but we'll find that there's no way that we can use anything Shimon Bar-El ever does for the benefit of Freiheim, or any other German colony."

Alon sighed. "Amazing that he was so effective, then."

Levine shook his head. "Not really. Most good fighting generals have their peccadilloes. I'd be tempted to say 'all,' but there's an exception or two."

You can dispute, if you want, whether or not Shimon should hold a grudge against modern humans of German ancestry, most of them as innocent as any other randomly-selected set of humans—which isn't much, really—all of them people whose grandparents' grandparents weren't even born until well after the First Holocaust . . .

. . . but argue it with *him*.

He did hold a grudge.

Shimon had always figured that Operation Theda Bara and

the events surrounding David's Gift had closed the books on the Second Holocaust and the Sunny Musselmen—they took Eretz Yisrael away from us, for now; David Bar-El took their Ka'aba and their religion away from them *forever*—but the First Holocaust never had been appropriately balanced.

Alon shrugged. It was evident who wasn't going to be sent to Nueva Terra if Metzada decided to hire on with the Freiheim side in the coming bloodletting.

Rivka caught my eye, looked at Ari, then looked at the door. Levine nodded.

It was an order. I'm not bad at obeying orders.

"Ari," I said, "you've got two wives and a bunch of children sitting around their apartment, wondering why their husband and father would rather spend time with others than with them. I'll see you at dinner."

He made no motion to rise. "If there's going to be an expedition to get Shimon out, I want in on it," he said.

"Request denied," Rivka Effron snapped. There was steel in her voice. "It will be a small team going to Thellonee, under cover of the negotiators. You're not qualified to lead, and I'm not going to let you play private. The closest you have to small-unit background is running company-sized assault teams."

Ari clenched his jaw.

"Ari." Alon held up a placating hand. "I'll be talking to DCSPERS tonight about your next assignment. And I'll see you at oh-eight-hundred tomorrow to talk about how we handle this FFL thing. That's got to be a high priority, all things considered."

"General—"

"Go home, Ari."

Generals, before they're ever generals, learn to settle for winning what battles they can: wordless, Ari rose and left.

When the door shut behind him, Zev snickered. "Pretty majestic, isn't he? Just what we need on an easy little snatch-and-run, a fucking hero."

"Shut up," Levine said flatly. "Tetsuo, our latest intelligence on Shimon is sketchy; we don't have any operatives in New

Portsmouth. All I can tell you for sure is that he's living near the port, in a fairly rundown section of New Portsmouth. He may be doing a bit of consulting on the side, but there are rumors that he's somehow involved in local criminal activity."

Rivka raised an eyebrow. "You don't seem surprised."

"True. And I'm not bothered, either." I wasn't surprised, and even if I was, I know better than to let it show. "I don't mind dealing with established criminals—the richer, the more powerful, the better. They have an address. So, say he's made himself too valuable to some underworld bigshot. If you give me enough support, I can probably get him out of that kind of situation, but what do we do then?"

"Can you?" Rivka Effron raised an eyebrow. "I don't trust this uncle of yours, and I'm not about to risk a team of expensively trained and highly valuable young soldiers on getting him out of whatever mess he's in. You can have a half dozen semi-retired veterans. Or retired ones, if you want. They'll be going in as career noncoms accompanying a negotiating team. I don't want a bunch of eighteen-year-old elite strikers trying to play clerk. Nobody's going to believe that."

It made sense. Most of what the old woman decides makes sense. "As long as I get my pick—"

"Volunteers, only."

I repressed a smile. The old woman is devious, wise, and subtle, but she doesn't understand quite everything. "And when I get him out?"

"*If* you get him out." Rivka Effron looked me in the eye. "How can you be sure you'll even find him?"

"Not a problem," Zev put in. "Assuming he wants to be found." He looked over at me. "What say we just make our presence known to every criminal type we can, and see what happens?"

I nodded. "Trick is to make sure we stay alive while we're bumping around, but it should work. He'll be findable." She was underestimating my uncle. As long as we kept it straightforward, we'd find him. "But when we do find him? What then?"

She seemed not to hear the question. "If he isn't lying, then he's got some sort of fix on some contract. Like he had on Indess."

"Almost certainly," Levine agreed. "If he isn't lying."

"Why?" Alon asked. "How can you be so sure? Couldn't he just be angling for another try at a command?"

Zev snorted. My partner never had a high opinion of generals. "You really eager to give him a command? Particularly after he outsmarted Rivka's favorite killer last time?" he went on, indicating me with a jerk of his thumb.

"No, but—"

"Of course not. And he knows it. And he also knows that it's going to be one of us headhunters coming out for him. Section isn't trained in complicated military planning. So it's going to be something simple, elegant."

I picked up the train of thought. "It's going to take more than twenty words to describe, but it's going to be something that he *knows* he can convince a Section killer is a good plan, even with some lesser mortal leading it. But he's not going to tell us until we've got him out of his predicament, if then. He might hold out until we're on the scene, wherever the scene is."

Zev nodded. "We find him; he tells us—assuming that he *will* tell us. We either refer it to you, or go ahead and implement it. What then?"

"I have had about enough of this Shimon Bar-El," Rivka said. "Find out what he knows, then fix it so that he isn't a problem for us anymore."

Alon nodded. "It's clearly necessary. He's a loose cannon."

"Pinhas?" I turned to Levine.

He sat silent for a long moment.

"There has long been," Pinhas Levine said, with a deep sigh, "a lot more knowledge locked up in his head than I like to think about. He's always known too much. He's managed to keep himself out of the wrong hands, so far, but . . ."

He shook his head. "Make it look like an accident."

CHAPTER
FOUR Salutes

The one-way glass at the front of the classroom looked out on both rooms: the smaller one that was labeled HALLWAY, with the directions of the entirely theoretical continuation of the hall chalked in on the far wall; and the larger one that contained a table, around which sat ten men. This one was labelled GENERAL STAFF ROOM.

Men, not boys: while they were all wearing the elegant black and silver uniforms that Freiheimer field-grade general staff officers used a war and a half ago—real uniforms, by the way; war prizes—the men gathered around the table in the room were in their fifties, one well into his sixties.

That's not unusual for us. There are countries, there are worlds, where good, albeit old soldiers are sent out to pasture, to sit uselessly and watch the days go by.

Good men die too early in those countries, on those worlds, both young soldiers and old ones. We still don't do enough for our old ones, granted, but we do have them teach our young how to not get killed unnecessarily. That's something.

73

In the HALLWAY, just outside the door, a twenty-year-old private in Metzadan khakis waited, a pair of goggles high on his forehead, in his hands a Barak assault rifle, its muzzle hooded by the orange cylinder of the fire simulator. His back was to the wall adjacent to the GENERAL STAFF ROOM; at his feet lay a dummy wearing a Freiheimer uniform and private's stripes.

At the top of the glass wall separating the classroom from the two other rooms beyond, a timer stood, poised at 1503.

The Sergeant stood at the front of the room, a pointer in his hand. He was pushing sixty and his khakis were cut amply to allow for his expanded belly.

But, underneath the honorable retirement pin on his chest, there were six rows of campaign ribbons.

We don't give out medals for bravery on Metzada, not to ourselves. Just campaign ribbons. The Sergeant had six rows of campaign ribbons, under the little gold Star of David pin that means a man is now retired, has completed all military obligations to Metzada.

The pin is intended to be an honorable award; the notion behind it is that we wouldn't make such jewelry if it could fall into enemy hands.

We, those of us who haven't gotten one yet, call it an honorable retirement pin.

The men who wear it call it something else entirely.

"Okay, now we're fifteen minutes into the assault, and he's taken out the guard. Next step?" He didn't pause in his questioning to greet me; he just gave me a quick nod and smile.

A skinny fourteen-year-old waved his hand frantically; the Sergeant ignored him and pointed to the round-faced, bored-looking boy sitting behind him. "Aaron?"

"I dunno." Aaron shrugged. "He should just kick open the door and throw in a grenade, then run like hell."

The Sergeant grinned. "Not a bad answer."

Aaron's face broke into a smile.

"Just a wrong one," the Sergeant said.

The boy's face fell.

"Still, let's give it a try," the Sergeant said. He picked up the microphone and announced, "Grenade assault, please. One grenade only—oh, and you kick the door down. Beginning timing in five seconds. Five. Four. Three. Two. *One.*"

The private pulled the goggles down. As he moved, the Sergeant slapped his hand down on the big red button on his desk; the timer started.

Transferring his rifle to his left hand, the private pulled a dummy grenade from his web belt, caught the pin on his belt hook, and pulled the grenade away from the pin, not letting go of the spoon. He kicked at the door—it took him two tries to get it to swing away—then threw in the grenade and ran the couple of feet down the hall until he reached the wall, where he ran in place, miming running along further.

The GENERAL STAFF ROOM suddenly went dark; the speaker on the wall announced, *"Moderate explosion behind soldier. He escapes down the hall uninjured, for at least the next ten seconds."*

"Freeze," the Sergeant said into his microphone, slapping at the red switch and stopping the timer at 1513. The private stopped running in place, slung his rifle, and leaned back against the wall, closing his eyes.

"Wait a minute—" Aaron raised his hand to protest. "How many did he kill?"

The Sergeant shrugged. "I don't know. Do you?"

"No. Somebody coulda thrown himself on the grenade."

Another boy laughed. "Yeah, yeah, you'd do that."

"Maybe," another boy said, "maybe he only got one or two of them. Maybe even none. They could have turned the table over and hidden behind it."

Another boy didn't like the whole thing. "I thought you said we usually can't get at a general staff."

The Sergeant nodded. "We're lucky if we ever get this kind of shot at even, say, a regimental staff."

"Then he should be sure that they're dead. I mean, it sounds like maybe I think I'm brave or something without anything to show it, but even if he gets killed, if he's killed off a regimental staff, it should be worth it to Metzada. And more so for a general staff, no?"

"Right. And very good, Levi. You're thinking in exactly the right terms." The Sergeant picked up the microphone. "Prepare to restart it," he said, resetting the clock.

He finally seemed to take notice of me. "I see we have Inspector-General Tetsuo Hanavi visiting the class today. He used to be a real soldier, before he joined the IG Corps. Remember your lessons, Tetsuo? You mind demonstrating another wrong way to do it?"

"Fine," I said, "but let's just simulate the door being kicked down. I have a bad knee."

"Will do." He threw me a pair of goggles. "Put them on."

"What for?"

"See, the thing of it is, I'm teaching this class, and you're not. That means that you get to do it my way," he said with a smile that he didn't entirely mean.

I put the goggles on, and he waved me toward the door leading into the hallway. I walked through, shut the door behind me, and relieved the private of his phony weapon. I checked the empty magazine and chamber as a matter of reflex before I slid the magazine out and then back in, resetting the fire simulator's counter.

"Now watch this carefully, class."

I took up his position to the side of the room, and raised the rifle to port position.

"Beginning timing on five," the overhead speaker announced. *"Five. Four. Three. Two. One."*

"Simulating kick," I said as I turned and gently kicked at the door; it swung open immediately, as though broken.

I stepped inside the staff room.

"Good evening, gentlemen," I said.

Two of the staff officers yelled; a third snatched at the pistol on his belt.

I just held down the trigger and sprayed imaginary fire all the way across the room, ignoring the simultaneous loud *crack*s of two simulated pistol shots, while the rifle went silent, simulating emptiness.

Their shots weren't quite as simulated as they used to be when I was a boy in school. One pellet slammed into the wall next to me, but the other caught me on the right side of my forehead, snapping my head back, sending a cool wetness sliding down the right side of my face.

I brought up my hand to my face; it came away red with fake blood. Now I understood the reason for the eye protection.

"Score: six out of ten men wounded, three dead, one unin- jured. Our striker is also dead. Now, pay attention: what mistakes did you make, General?"

"One." I stripped the goggles off and held up a finger as I turned, letting them see what a bloody face looked like.

Not really the way it was, but as the lights came up in the classroom, I could see from the pale faces that the point had gotten through.

"Kicking open a door when you haven't even quietly tried the knob is pretty silly. It just announces that something violent is about to happen, and can draw attention from other quarters. If you know the local knock, and can talk the local language, much better to just knock, announce yourself, and walk in."

"Two."

"Two: I had the burst suppressor off, and I sprayed around the room like I was using an autogun to sweep a beaten-fire zone. That would have been a bad mistake. An assault rifle has a limited clip—I should have set it for five-round bursts, then picked targets and walked the bursts through them."

"Priorities?"

"My first target should have been the man who was mov- ing; he was clearly the most dangerous adversary.

"Second and third," I went on, "should have been the ones yelling; they understood what was going on, and were the next most dangerous. That would have taken about twenty rounds, altogether—including an extra insurance burst.

"After that, I should have remembered that the Barak assault rifle has only thirty rounds in the clip, and disengaged from the room, firing another burst while I did so, which would have left me five rounds to deal with anything unexpected in the corridor. Then I could toss in a grenade while I reloaded."

"What is the worst thing you did?"

"The 'Good evening, gentlemen.' That was ridiculous. I was there to kill them, not to talk to them."

"True."

I wiped the phony blood from my face and waved my wet hand at the Sergeant. "You got something I can use to wash this off?"

I was towelling at my wet hair while, behind the plexi, the old soldiers who had been playing at being Freiheimers were busy rearranging the room for the next class.

"Very nice," the Sergeant said. "I see that you remember your lessons."

A bit. One of the things I did, in my spare time, was to teach the Section version of an entry-and-assault, which is a bit more demanding: we're supposed to be able to move in and out a lot more quietly than regular soldiers.

But I remembered the basics, the ones you teach to line troops.

I nodded. "The question is, Uncle Tzvi, is this all just practice, or do you still have it? And do you have five friends?"

He was silent for a long moment. Then:

"For what?" he asked, as if it mattered. He knew what I was offering; he would do whatever I asked him to do, and he knew it damn well.

I shrugged, as though I was considering, then dismissing, his concern. "To spring Shimon Bar-El out of whatever problem he's in on Thellonee. Hope it's a small problem, because there's going to be less than a dozen of us, altogether, and we're going under cover of a negotiating team—I don't want to use any of the real negotiators. No weapons, except for whatever we can procure locally."

"On Thellonee? That's going to be a bitch."

I shrugged. "No pretenses between you and me: it's likely to be bloody, Uncle. We'll start it off with the Mercenary's Toast, but it'll be a lie."

" 'The Mercenary's Toast is a wish, not a promise.' " The Sergeant smiled. "I think that can be worked out. Only promise I need from you, is that if I do well enough on this, you'll consider using me again. For something where the goal is something better than this."

Shimon was my mother's brother; Tzvi Hanavi, my father's. Little love was lost between the two of them; Uncle Tzvi would have cut off his own hand before betraying Metzada.

Still, this wouldn't be about rescuing Shimon Bar-El. It would be about blood.

The wars drive us all insane. Some men are broken into useless hulks that can't even feed themselves. Some men get a taste for blood. The Sergeant was one of those. I'd just given him a whiff of it. He'd follow the scent all the way to Thellonee, as long as I let him, as long as I led him. It wouldn't even matter if I told him that I was deliberately manipulating him.

He wouldn't care.

"No promises," I said. "Now, can you find some friends? Or do you want me to fill out the team?"

"What kind of friends?" he said, again with a smile. It was a real smile, but it wasn't an amused one.

"Old ones. Expendable. Retired. Blooded. The kind of men that it's easy to underrate, but who still have a little something left, even if they can't run as hard as they could when they were boys."

His smile wasn't friendly anymore. "Expendable old soldiers for an expendable mission? What expendable idiot is running it?"

"Me."

"You? Correct me if I'm wrong, little Tetsuki, but have you *ever* had a command? You were a staff officer until they made you IG."

I touched a finger to the star on my left shoulder. "This says

I'm considered qualified to command an offplanet mission, all by myself. You want in or out?"

His smile ceased being that of a hunting tiger, and became the sad one of an old man who felt more than a little useless. "Any good news?"

"I think I can get Dov in on the team."

"No. That wasn't what I meant. I mean, it is important?"

I shrugged. "I don't know. I think it may be, but I don't know."

"But you think so?"

"I think so."

The smile broadened. "In."

As though my saying it might be important had made a difference. The old tiger would have been in anything that meant action, anything that meant another taste of warm blood in his mouth, even if it was his own.

He nodded again. "You'll have your retread soldiers, Tetsuo; I'll get started now. When do we leave?"

"One week."

"Good."

"Why is that good?"

"In another two weeks," he said, smiling as he clapped a strong hand to my shoulder, "'I might be too old for this. I'd best get to work. One would think that there isn't much time to get another five old useless men."

"How long do you figure it'll take? All you can say is that it's a mission, and that they are to consider themselves expendable."

For a moment, we were pupil and teacher again, and he was again disappointed with me for not paying attention to the words of yesterday's lesson. I could see my father in his eyes. My father never approved of me.

"Tetsuo, Tetsuo . . . you forget, sometimes," he said, with my father's voice. "Remember Eleazar ben Mattityahu?"

What's colloquially known as a kamikaze attack—a suicidal attack by a single man on a capital asset of the enemy—was *not* invented in Earth's Second World War by the Nipponese. Our people had invented it millenia before, when the Maccabees kicked the shit out of the Assyrians, sending the bastards running home.

The Assyrians had elephant cavalary—large, destructive beasts, easily two men tall—that could crash through our lines, crushing whatever was in their way, scattering the rest. The sides of the animal were always armored, and it had a trunk—a long, snakelike protuberance growing out of its face—to protect itself from a frontal attack.

There was only one way to stop an elephant, and Eleazar, son of Mattityahu, brother to Yehuda the Hammer, found it: he stood still and let one of the beasts come over him, knocking him flat to his back.

And then he thrust his spear upwards, into its soft underbelly. The elephant collapsed on the spot.

Eleazar was the spot.

"I don't see the connection."

"Fuck you, General. Like hell you don't." Tzvi Hanavi picked up his microphone. "Zachariah," he said, "go home. Your grandchildren need to see you." The thin, silver-haired man shrugged, nodded, and left.

The Sergeant looked through the glass and dismissed five others, leaving behind five men, ranging in age from perhaps as young as fifty to Yehuda Nakamura, who I knew was sixty. Don't let his Nipponese name mislead you; old Yehuda has a little Nipponese blood as I do, but the Nakamuras kept their patronym when they joined clan Aroni.

"Eleazar ben Mattityahu is calling you," Tzvi Hanavi said, to what I suddenly realized was all that was left of his old company. Blunt fingers came up to his honorable retirement pin, and tore it away from his uniform shirt. It dropped to the floor. "You'd better plan on reporting in uniform tomorrow at oh-eight-hundred—and you can lose those fucking we-don't-need-you-anymore pins."

"We can *what*?" one asked.

"You heard him, he said we can lose the fucking we-don't-need-you-anymore pins."

The Sergeant hugged me. When he pressed his cheek against

mine, it was wet. "Tetsuki," he said, "thank you. I thought I was going to die in this fucking rock."

As he released me, five old men gathered around us, all of them half out of the Freiheimer uniforms, none of them wearing anything from the waist up but their undershirts. Not very prepossessing, to look at. They were all slack-bellied, skins whitened from too many years in Metzada.

"Tzvi?" Thin, bald Menachem Yabotinsky asked. "Are you serious?"

"Yeah," the Sergeant said. "You in, or do I need to find another corporal?"

Yabotinsky barely smiled. "In."

"Besides, he wouldn't shit us about something like this," white-haired Yehoshua Bernstein said. "Is it still okay to be scared?" He looked older than he was, and was clearly the frailest of all of them, but if he was good enough for the Sergeant, I hoped he'd be good enough.

"Fuck, yes," Ephriam Imran said. "For me, this is almost enough to put lead back in my pencil."

"C'mon, Eph." Yehuda Nakamura snickered. "Take a hell of a lot from your medikit to put lead back in—"

"Shut up and line up," Tzvi said, and he and Yabotinsky glared them into order.

"It's purely a voluntary assignment," I said. "Nobody's under any compulsion to volunteer."

It wasn't as though what I said was heard and decidedly ignored; it was as though I was broadcasting on a frequency that they weren't equipped to receive.

The Sergeant performed a sharp right face and drew himself up to attention as he faced me.

"General," he said, as he turned back to me, "Sergeant Tzvi Hanavi, with elements of Company C, First Battalion, the Old Eighteenth Regiment, reporting for duty, *sir*."

Then he threw me a salute, and held it.

We're not much on saluting in Metzada; it took me aback.

" 'A salute,' " he said, when I didn't react, " 'is not a bow. A bow is a gesture from a subordinate to a superior. A salute is a

greeting between practitioners of the profession of arms, one
that is initiated by the junior, and returned by the senior.' You
have six practitioners of the profession of arms in front of you,
sir. You have six soldiers."

"That I do." I returned the salute. "Carry on, Sergeant."

CHAPTER FIVE Family Affair

Home to me has never meant whatever bed or compartment I've been assigned to. Those have kept changing; besides, a soldier ought to learn not to be particular about where he sleeps.

Home has always meant Refectory Gimel, the huge, open room where laughter occasionally peeks through the curtain of murmured conversation.

Refectory Gimel isn't just where I eat when I'm home; it's also where my family is. Both times I was married, it was in Refectory Gimel, with four thousand of my family shouting their wishes for our happiness.

It was where my father Yisrael used to preside at our family table, over our portion of the Passover service, in true Bar-El clan fashion. When the religious celebrate Sabbath or Passover, they cover even their butter knives while they pray, as though to shield God's gaze from what knives symbolize. We do things differently in clan Bar-El, reading from the Haggadah as we celebrate the exodus from Egypt, bared knives and loaded assault rifles piled on the table, giving meaning to the final words: "And so shall we remain free men!"

Refectory Gimel is also where the clan board is, covering half the western wall. I couldn't read it from where I sat, but I had glanced at it before supper: the status of the new Eighteenth had just been updated, and Benyamin was still well.

Supper that night was about as usual, except for the extra merriment at Ari's table, next to mine. At mine there was a bit of added tension, caused in part by an extra absence.

Although . . . I didn't like the proportions on the plates. You can tell a lot about how Metzada is doing by the size of the portions on the supper trays. There had been a lot more rice cake than chicken cutlet tonight.

Benyamin's chair would have been empty, but it had been taken by Devorah Amrani, his (in my opinion) overly-quiet, fifteen-year-old fiancée, who was visiting for the evening. Probably to spend time with my daughter Z'porah, who was the same age, as much as to mingle with the rest of the family.

Rachel wiped at little Devorah's—a different Devorah; our year-old daughter—mouth with a damp washcloth, then tried to force more strained beets in.

Rachel wasn't having a whole lot of luck; as much seemed to ooze out as went in; I suspect young children actually absorb nutrients through their cheeks. Rachel didn't share my suspicion; she blew a stray strand of hair from her forehead and tried again, turning to help two-year-old Shlomo manhandle his carrots.

Yes, Shlomo, there is another Shlomo among the Hanavis. I may not have liked my brother, but I did love him.

"How they manage to feed them in creche, I'll never understand," Rachel said.

"Be grateful," I said, "that you only have them for one meal a day." I would have offered to help, but I probably wasn't any better at it than she was.

There were tables where I was not popular. A few tables away, where the Sergeant presided over his three wives, all his children long since grown and moved away, two out of the three women were taking turns glaring at me.

Sorry, Aunties, I wanted to say. *But I need him.*

Metzada needed him. I might have even put forward some nonsense about him being a volunteer, but that had never been a consideration. The lesson of Eleazar ben Mattityahu is not always what it appears to be; consider his brother, Yehuda. . . .

But, still, the room was festive. Many Bar-El men were home, some of them, like my brother Ari, who was holding court at the table next to mine, actually starting to relax.

We had a small, eight-person table at that point; there were seven of us at full complement. Yet another Devorah, my stepdaughter, had just married a month before, and was a quarter-klick across the refectory, at table with her in-laws.

"Za-za," I said, using Z'porah's baby nickname, "help your mother with Shlomo."

Za-za sniffed, as though to say, *she isn't my mother and you aren't my father,* both of which would have been true, in a sense, but both likely to get her in trouble. One of the first things you learn when you take your second wife is that children will try to play one off against the other, and that that must not be tolerated.

Devorah Amrani's downcast eyes kept shifting to other tables, probably sorting out eligible bachelors.

I held back a frown at that. She and Benyamin were not yet married, and he wasn't yet back from his first time offworld. Alsace, too. I wished he'd lucked into something a bit easier. I hadn't seen a report from Alsace for a week, but things were not going well. A complicated situation, really: their extra mobility was allowing the Dutch Confederate forces to carve right through French line defenses. Yonni Davis' new Eighteenth was enough to stop a French advance anywhere they were, but a regiment can only be in one place at one time, unless you go for a dispersal, which is unsuitable for point defense.

I shrugged. Tactics and strategy are not my forte, but they

were Yonni's. Hopefully, he'd figure something out, and if he didn't, then I certainly couldn't.

Suki's chair, at the other end of our table, was empty; she was still in surgery, and had sent word that she wasn't to be expected home until about 0300—if everything went okay.

"What else did she say?" I asked.

"That she checked on Dov," Rachel said. "And that he's out of surgery and resting fine, but had demanded a phone."

Dov was stretched out on his bed in the infirmary, just one of a long line of patients that almost vanished into the distance. We are not a rich world; private rooms are for the contagious.

There is a solid quiet in the hospital, an almost verbal lack of noise that's more punctuated than interrupted by the slap of the attendants' shoes on the hard floors, the whir of a pump, or the hacking cough and whispered voices of the sick.

Dov looked like hell. There was a tube running up his nose, a bag of something or other dripping into his veins, and his eyes seemed to have trouble focusing, but as he lay in his drab, gray patient's gown he still looked anything but innocuous. Behind his ashen complexion, he was still Dov.

"Visiting, sir?" he asked, his voice raw around the edges. He swallowed twice.

"Just seeing how you're doing," I said as I pulled up a chair. Suki might not have known, not really; an appendectomy is far too minor an operation for her to do herself, even if she was going to be physician of record.

"There apparently were some complications, sir," he said. "I was told I will not be fit to travel for at least ten days."

He was taking that too well. "So what did you tell the doctor?"

"I called the deputy, sir," he said. "I told her that I was going to Thellonee with the rest of you."

"And she said?"

"After a short discussion, sir, she agreed that I was, and she talked to the doctor, and I begin NoGain therapy in the morning."

I shuddered. NoGain magnifies your pain, and Dov had been cut into. You can't dull exposed nerve endings with valda oil, either; the two drugs interact, and the only thing I know about it is that the result is not potentiation.

"It's necessary, sir," he said. "If I am to travel with you. Regardless of the expense." His own pain wasn't a matter for discussion, or for consideration. It wasn't important to Shimon.

"What exactly did you tell her?"

He returned my gaze levelly. "Shimon once told me that there might come a time when I would decide that I ought to try to join him, sir. He gave me specific instructions in case either Rivka Effron or you were the ones blocking me from doing that, and general instructions in case it was someone else. He told me what to say."

"And that was?"

"Nothing subtle, sir. I wasn't ordered to be subtle. Just that I would be allowed to join Shimon, or I would be killed by Rivka Effron's guards before or after I killed her. Before she could say anything, I pointed out that since I truly meant that, and since her guards could easily take me in my present condition, it made me militarily useless, and completely expendable for this assignment."

"Shimon told you to say that?"

"If injured or sick, yes. Word for word, sir." He nodded slowly. "I always do what he says. I always have."

What happened next may have been the drugs and the exhaustion. Even with a constitution like Dov's, being operated on takes something out of you, opens up channels of weakness that you might have not thought were there.

"I was a weak little boy, when the soldiers came," Dov said, as though to himself. "He changed that."

I don't know enough about it, but Shimon's Children's Crusade began when Shimon Bar-El, then a private, alone and cut off from his company, ran across a group of soldiers torching an orphanage, raping the girl children, killing the boys. I don't exactly know what happened next, but the upshot was that Shimon and his new underage troops carved their way through Neuheim territory back to our lines, leaving death and destruction in their wake, arriving dirty, battered, tired, and bloody, with only six of the original two hundred children alive.

The ten-year-old boy he called Dov was one of the six.

I once saw a flat picture taken that afternoon, of that spindly ten-year-old boy, still hefting one of those oversized autoguns the Neuheimers like to burden their infantrymen with. The boy was wearing little except rags and a necklace of what looked, at first glance, like dozens of figs. They were souvenirs, of a sort.

"What did he do, Dov?" I asked.

"Something he said." He smiled weakly and then shrugged. "You wouldn't understand; you weren't there." Dov Ginsberg closed his eyes. "I have to sleep now."

CHAPTER
SIX Farewells

The story is told of a famous sword maker who was approached by a would-be student. "How long, sensei," the student asked, "will I have to study in order to learn the art of swordmaking?"

"Ten years," the teacher said.

"But I will study night and day!" the student exclaimed.

"In that case, twenty years."

"Then let me devote every attention to it, concentrating all my energies on learning the art, pushing every fiber of my being to the maximum to learn the art of swordmaking."

"In that case, it will take you thirty years," the teacher said, returning to his anvil.

I used to practice Zen because I thought it would give me insight. And then I stopped getting insight and started to learn the Arts.

No, that's too complicated. It's much simpler, really: the sages used to insist that a rabbi must have another way of earning money; the Akiva himself, we are taught, was a common laborer. Why? Because Torah is not a shovel; Torah is too important to be a way to make a living.

The Arts aren't a shovel, either, although sometimes we have to use them like a headsman's axe. When we do, it should feel like sacrilege, like hitting someone over the head with the Torah scroll.

It doesn't, not for me.

So much the worse for me.

The room doesn't exist. Warrens and wings are named; sections begin with One, compartments with Aleph. There have been maps smuggled off Metzada, by the occasional offworlder we allow in Metzada. All of them show named warrens and wings, section numbers starting with One, compartments with Aleph.

Follow the syllogism: since Section is Section 0, Section doesn't exist.

Neither do I. You don't exist, either. Everything is, is not, will be, will ever not be. All is illusion.

An arc of ten men, each clad in a worn gi, ranging in ages from seventeen to almost seventy, knelt on simple mats of surface grass. Not all of Section, of course. Not even all on-planet. Just those who were there that night.

Ten is a special number for us. There were ten lost tribes, ten commandments, ten is minyan.

Halfway across the circle from me Zev knelt, his dark face impassive, not with strict control of emotions, I think, but with mind like water, mind like the moon, the mind that sees everything, but lets all wash over it. Zev was farther along than I was.

Even with the whir of the air conditioners, the room was stifling, the air so humid that the rough rock walls glistened in the warm light of the overhead glows. It is impossible to practice without raising a sweat, and all of us had been working out for a solid two hours, fists flying in seiken and uraken, open hands thrusting and slashing in shuto, feet moving in geri and keage.

There is something special, something beautiful in what happens in the dojo; I've always felt that to have to bring any of it outside is only to soil it with blood. The beauty is in the thing itself.

At the focus of the arc sat Pinhas Levine.

Ten minutes' rest would have been enough to loosen tired muscles; a full night's would not have been enough for me to completely recover from the exercise.

We sat zazen for more than an hour before he spoke.

I do not practice the Arts because they make me a better person; they don't. I don't practice the Arts because it somehow makes my vision clearer; I've always seen everything and nothing. I don't practice the Arts to make myself wise; I'm already a fool and a sage, who knows all and understands nothing.

The universe is a cruel joke, but cruelty is kindness.

Ignorance is truth.

Trust me on this one: in truth, we are all ignorant.

War is peace; George Orwell should have studied the Arts. He would have been just the same as he was before he started, if he studied it long enough and well enough—but not *hard* enough. He would have had to study without trying.

"Metzada is a cold rock," Pinhas said, beginning without preamble or warning, his voice barely above a whisper, although I had no trouble hearing his every syllable. "Still, it preserves. The religious preserve the Law; stories told in the refectories after supper keep the families strong; the army keeps Am Yisroel, the people of Israel, from dying.

"We preserve something else here, something that's valuable, too." His lips quirked into a smile. "In its own way."

He said it with the quiet practiced patience a man can use when he says something he believes fully, if not unquestioningly, when he takes that belief out only to display it to others who value it.

I've heard that tone elsewhere, seen that expression in few other places. If you happen to be up at the pulpit for an aliyah, you may be lucky enough to see it in his face for a moment when a devout rebbe, the meaning of what he does fully upon him, takes out the Torah and holds it over his head as he turns his back to the Ark. He turns his back to the Ark not out of disrespect, but so that the rest of his congregation can see the words, share the writing.

What Pinhas was doing was like that. We'd all heard before what he had to say, although he always phrased it differently, but there's something special, something almost loving, in the repetition.

"What we do here isn't just to teach ourselves to kill better. We're preserving ways that were almost lost, that would have been lost, if the madmen of the Bushido Brotherhood hadn't kept them alive, and brought them to Metzada to be preserved and protected until they can be returned to Nippon. Right now, I don't know if the Nipponese want the Arts back, and I'm not going to ask. It's not time for that, not yet.

"In the meantime, the Arts can serve us." He shrugged. "If not, we'd probably have to let them die off." He looked at me, but he was talking to the others. "Two of us are now leaving Metzada—yet again."

He rose, walked to a cabinet at the front of the room, and opened it. It was unlocked.

From it, he took a rolled cloth and returned to the circle of men, seating himself across from me. He unrolled the black cloth and spread out the instruments inside. "Tetsuo, if you want to, you may take any of this with you, with the understanding that it can be used as necessary, but not exposed to the sight of the gaijin."

It's one thing to be good at hand-to-hand; that's permissible, even expected, from a soldier. But the rest of the Art is hidden; it's always been that way.

"You can take these with you, but on your own responsibility," Pinhas said. "The decision is yours."

Old Yehuda Agron looked over at me, his eyes missing nothing. "Tetsuo, you are . . . ?"

I shrugged. "I am worried, Adoni, worried."

His eyes twinkled; his fingers, seemingly of their own will, twisted themselves in his long beard. "Ah. You feel that these are not quite the right weapons? Maybe you would rather have a better mind than a few shuriken?"

I forced a smile.

"I don't blame you," he said. "You're wiser than I was at your age. When I was in my thirties, I thought that there was no problem in the universe that couldn't be solved by slitting the right throat."

Levine almost glared at him, but the old man wouldn't have cared, so he didn't. My boss is always studied in everything he does. It's one of the reasons I respect him.

"You think your uncle knows you better than you know him?" the old one asked.

"Perhaps." I rubbed my hands across my face. "Sometimes, I feel like it's going to be a duel of wits between Shimon and me, and I'm the unarmed opponent."

"We can't give you wit, boy. And if you don't know where to point them, weapons are pointless. A good joke, eh?"

"Not particularly," I said.

"I'm a retired headsman, Tetsuo, not a comedian." He rose and lightly folded the cloth over the instruments, then handed the bundle to Pinhas. "Put them away, Pinhas," he said, then turned back to me. "The battle isn't over your uncle, but with him. Don't let yourself be distracted, not by anything. Do what you have to do. Whatever that is," he said. "Whatever that is."

Pinhas looked from face to face. Even among ourselves, we compartment, segment some knowledge, and slap walls labeled "Need to Know" between our minds, between ourselves.

"Need to know," I said.

As though it were a great joke, old Yehuda laughed, and other faces broke into smiles.

"Ah, ah," he said, tears streaming down his cheeks, losing themselves in his ragged beard, "you keep such secrets, Tetsuo Hanavi, such secrets. And you, Pinhas, you're such an asshole. You tell Tetsuo to kill his uncle and you expect it not to show here? You expect me not to see it?"

Levine let himself smile. "One can always hope."

Old Yehuda turned to me. "Are you paying attention, Tetsuki?"

"You haven't asked me that for years."

"True." He nodded. "I'm asking you now: are you paying attention, Tetsuki?"

"Always, Adoni, always."

Outside, in the real world, it would have mattered that something I had said, or something that Pinhas had said or done, had told the others what my orders were.

But here, it didn't matter.

It was suddenly all a joke. It didn't matter. Nothing matters, and everything matters.

I threw back my head and laughed.

The times in the dojo are good ones, I think.

I slept with only Suki that night; Rachel had creche duty.

In the morning, I rose and dressed.

The family creche is one corridor over and two levels down from our apartment. It took me only a few minutes to walk over, bag slung over my shoulder.

Rachel's eyes were puffy with white-night sleepiness as she sat at the desk outside the four-year-olds' creche. She rose and clung to me.

"I'll miss you," she said.

"As will I, you," I said, perhaps too formally, holding her tightly. I think we've been together too long; we were married when I was just sixteen; she was fourteen. Eighteen years is a long time. Too long to really be strangers, too little time for us to ever get to really know each other. I know every inch of Rachel's body, but I really don't know her. And she really doesn't know me.

I think she's better for that; just as well she doesn't know me.

"You've already seen Shlomo?"

"Not yet."

"Well, I don't want you in there. We've had a rough night; she's—"

"I won't disturb anything."

"No."

You can't pull rank on your wife.

I kissed her goodbye, long and hard. As she pulled away from me, she looked at me curiously. "This *is* just routine, isn't it?"

I nodded, lying. Rachel has never quite worked out what I do, and I didn't want to worry her. "Just part of a negotiating team, that's all. Maybe a side trip or two, but nothing heavy."

"Well, good." She *tsk*ed. "You be careful, then. I don't like the way you keep being around when there's shooting."

I stopped at the two-year-olds' creche and bullied sleepy-eyed cousin Sarai into letting me in.

"I won't disturb them, I promise," I said, as I set down my bag and slipped off my shoes.

She didn't say anything; she just glared at me.

I opened the door.

The Arts have some minor applications; I shut the door behind me, and became Silence.

That's the real secret. It isn't the technique, although that's where you have to start: weight always balanced easily on the balls of the feet, each foot lifted and set down, under control, not merely allowing yourself to stagger through life, the way most people do.

No, it's not just technique. It's the becoming. All the Art is, is becoming. Silence is one of the easier things to become; it doesn't trouble you later.

I drifted through the room until I was at Shlomo's crib.

He slept easily, his little knees pulled up underneath him, one chubby arm outflung, the other tucked in closely. I put my hand lightly to the back of his head, and wondered, for the thousandth time, why it is that God makes my children of such special stuff, why the hair on the back of my children's heads is always softer, finer than that He uses for the rest of his Creation.

I love you, little one, I mouthed.

There was a time in my people's history, when a son might

inherit a civilian profession from his father. In one line of my family, there was an unbroken string of six generations of male doctors—real physicians, not just medicians; in another, a hundred years of rabbis.

All I have to leave to you is my profession. You can become a butcher like your father.

They were all waiting for me at the 'port. Dov, Zev, the Sergeant, and his oldsters, now in khakis that had no trace of honorable retirement pins, were over on one side of the room, Alon and his half-dozen assorted staff negotiation officers on the other.

At my arrival, Alon nodded and opened a cabinet at the far wall, bringing out a tray of shot glasses and a mottled stone bottle, complete with ceramic cork.

He squealed the cork out of the bottle and poured each of us a glass. "Gentlemen," he said, "I am the senior here. And who is the junior?"

"I am," Dov said, his voice normal once more: flat, almost too high-pitched, emotionless. He raised his glass. "Brothers and cousins, I give you the Mercenary's Toast."

"The Mercenary's Toast," we all echoed, as custom required.

"Everybody comes back," he said. No special intonation; he just said the words. It's a toast, not a prayer.

"Everybody comes back."

We drank the harsh whiskey. As the fiery liquid burned the back of my throat, I lowered the glass and set it down, empty, on the table.

And I remembered what the Sergeant used to murmur, back in the old days.

I didn't have to trust my memory, though; he turned to his six comrades and whispered, just like in the old days, "Remember, chaverim—it's a toast, not a promise."

PART TWO THELLONEE

When they brought forth the five kings before Joshua, Joshua called for all the men of Israel, and said to the war chiefs: "Come near, put your feet on the necks of these kings."

And they came near, and they put their feet on the necks of the kings. And Joshua said to them: "Fear not, be not dismayed, be strong and of good courage, for this is what the lord will do to all your enemies against whom you fight."

And afterward, Joshua put the kings to death, and hanged them on five trees.

—Joshua 10:24–26

CHAPTER SEVEN Guilty Pleasures

Thellonee, New Britain
New Portsmouth Port Facility
01/10/44, 1923 local time

We gathered in the living room of the penthouse complex in the northwestern arm of the New Portsmouth Hyatt.

It was only surrounded by New Portsmouth, not in it; the hotel was safely within the TW Preserve, protected by the powerfence and the towers at the preserve's perimeter. These days, that protection was more a matter of simple security than anything else; but there had been riots, back when New Britain was a penal colony.

Alon, his six officers and I were in mess dress, preparing to go down to the manager's reception and play negotiator. The Sergeant and his five oldsters were in mufti, all of them gathered around the dinner table over by the picture window.

I walked to the window and looked out into the night, past the weak spatter of raindrops against the glass.

Beyond the occasional flashes of the powerfence, the hulk of a dying city waited, maybe for some savior to breathe life back in it, more likely for some bulldozers to finish it off. Local brick might last two hundred years, but the four-, five- and six-story buildings at the edge of the city seemed ready to crumble at a look.

There had been a time when some of the most desirable property was near the port, but as the city had grown up around it, and clogged it, the heart of New Portsmouth had deteriorated. I've seen it before. More often, it happens around hospitals, although on a smaller scale. The buildings intended to heal the sick slowly turn into a barely safe zone in an expanse of filth and crime, like a single clean spot on a grease-spattered floor.

Off in the distance, I could see street lights trying to pierce the gloom, but they weren't trying very hard, and I didn't blame them.

"You should try some of this," the Sergeant said, speaking around a mouthful. "Best ham I've had in five years."

"It's the *first* ham you've had in five years," round-faced Ephraim Imran said.

"So, it has to be the best, no?" the Sergeant answered, rewarded by the thin but deep chuckles evoked by an old joke, taken out to be passed around and shared for a moment.

The Law is strictly enforced in Metzada, but it is understood that when we are off of Metzada, the rules don't apply.

Which is why Tzvi Hanavi and four of his oldsters were gathered around the table, gorging themselves on forbidden delicacies ordered from room service. Tzvi had finished with his bacon cheeseburger, and was helping Yehudah Nakamura with his huge order of ham and eggs. White-haired Yehoshua Bernstein was using a hunk of bread to mop up the milk gravy from his platter of veal chops; Ephraim Imran and Moshe Stern, both having finished their blood-rare steaks, sat back and drank cup after cup of cafe au lait. Imran belched while Stern drummed his fingers on the arm of his chair, puffing nervously on his tabstick in between sips.

The only one not eating was thin, balding Menachem Yabotinsky, who sat nervously in his chair, stubby fingers steepled in front of him, eyes missing nothing. He turned to put out a barely-lit tabstick, and immediately fired up another.

Two of the others had tabsticks burning in ashtrays. Damn silly habit, really, but one you can easily catch, off Metzada.

"So, you going to have some?" the Sergeant asked again.

"Maybe later," I said. "After the manager's reception. I don't want to muss the finery."

I don't eat a lot of tref; I have my own guilty pleasures to indulge outside of Metzada.

Mess dress doesn't have any pockets on the shirt or jacket; stooping, I pulled up the cuff of one trouser leg to pull my own pack from my sock, extracted one, thumbed it to life, then stuck it in the corner of my mouth while I replaced the pack. I straightened, and took a longer draw on the tabstick. The smoke was rich and satisfying; they grow good tobacco on Thellonee.

Still a damn silly habit.

Captain Aaron Gevat, Alon's logistics aide, walked up to me. "Check me over?"

"Sure."

In Metzada, we really don't go in for stylish uniforms *per se*; Metzadan khakis vary in thickness—and color; not all uniforms we call khakis are khaki—depending on the climatic, not social, conditions they're designed to be worn in, from the ten-weight desert khakis with mesh undershirt and short sleeves, to the multi-layered, sandwich-armored, chameleon-colored type C's that will keep you miserably cold but alive at minus forty.

On the other hand, for purposes other than fighting and training, sometimes you need more decorative uniforms. At least, that's what David Bar-El, nee Warcinsky, had been taught before he walked away from the Long Gray Line.

Other armies have a whole range of dress wear, ranging from the four or five levels of formal and sort-of-formal uniforms that the Thousand Worlds peacemakers wear, all the way to the twenty different subtleties of formal dress that the Casas sport. Some of them look like characters in an Italian opera. It's silly, mind, but don't hold that against them. A few assholes to the contrary—and what army would be complete without a few assholes?—the Casas are good folks.

We do things differently. We have one kind of formal uniform, called mess dress.

I pitched my tabstick at the oubliette and gestured at Gevat to turn around. I had to admit that he looked resplendent in mess dress. A short jacket, his in the blue of Infantry, mine in the gleaming white of the IG, was worn over a white vest, that over an almost gleaming white shirt with a winged collar. His sleeves were decorated with loops of golden cord—three, indicating that he was a captain—marked with flecks of black, showing that he held a senior warrant.

I may be above most of the nonsense, but I do have to admit that I like looking down at the arms of my mess dress and seeing seven elegant loops of gold braid on each sleeve, a single star at the wrist.

We are silly, we humans, caring about a loop of gold or a little metal star, or a few pieces of ribbon. Sometimes I wonder about us. About me.

The left breast of Gevat's tunic was covered with three rows of silken campaign ribbons, under which were his medals—not the miniatures that most armies prescribe for wear with formal uniforms. Metzada doesn't aware medals—except for the Two Swords, which is only awarded to offworlders serving under Metzadan officers—but we're not prohibited from accepting those of others.

My brother has quite a few; it's one of the perks that comes from being a line officer. The Casas gave him the Order of St. Augustine, which they pass out almost as rarely as we hand out the Two Swords. Gevat had a Legion of Merit, a Tae Guk, and a George's Cross.

"Got a loose thread on the shoulder here," I said. Thumbing a fresh tabstick to life, I took a long pull and considered the ash for a moment before I touched it to the thread. It shriveled like a snake in the wash of a flamethrower.

I threw my cape back over my shoulders—I hate the damn thing—and straightened myself for Gevat's final inspection before belting my sash more tightly around my hips, and sticking my daisho into its folds, both swords with their cutting edges facing rearward and up, as tradition demands. I don't believe in wearing weapons just for decoration, and the antiquity of my pair can sometimes be a handy technicality when trying to get through TW Customs onto low-tech worlds.

Gevat hitched at his swordbelt, then gave a quick polish to the silver guard of his saber. I'm not sure when the tradition of wearing swords on formal occasions returned, but it does tend to keep people polite. "You look fine, Tetsuo."

I caught Alon's eye, and held up a single finger. He nodded fractionally. "Be right back," I said.

I stepped out into the hall and went to Zev's rooms. I knocked twice. "It's me," I said.

The door opened. Zev and Dov were already dressed, in baggy gripsuits of different styles, different shades of dull gray, Dov's mainly covered by a taupe trailcoat that fell to his knees. They looked more than a little ragged around the edges.

"You two ready?" They both nodded.

"Almost," Zev amended. "I took some more Motrin, but I've still got a bit of the runs." He disappeared into the toilet and closed the door behind him.

"I am ready, sir." Dov had an old Korriphila Ten Thousand in a breakaway holster under his left armpit. He pulled the weapon from the leather and pumped a round into the chamber before removing the clip, adding an extra round to it, and putting that back in the weapon with a solid *chick*.

I was going to say something about how it was against standing orders to smuggle weapons off Metzada, and go into some detail about how the importation of firearms to Thellonee was strictly controlled, but if Dov was heeled, it was on Shimon's orders. There was no sense in wasting my breath.

I started to say something like *be careful,* but it would have been talking for the sake of hearing myself talk.

"Go easy on the violence. We don't want trouble. We just want to find out where Shimon is and what he's doing."

"Understood, sir," he said.

"How *did* you smuggle it in?" I asked.

He shrugged. "I didn't. Last time I was on Thellonee, I took it and two spare clips off of a mugger, then cached them. Weapons controls weren't so tight, then. It was still taped to the top of a pipe under a suspended ceiling over in the Trade towers."

I couldn't think of anything else important to say, and I've never made small talk with Dov, so we just stood quietly for a few minutes until, preceded by the sound of running water, Zev came out of the toilet, drying his hands on a fluffy towel.

"All ready?"

He tossed the towel aside. "Ready."

"Fine. Be careful. We need information, not body counts."

Zev nodded. He never minded being told the obvious. "Just don't be late at the rendezvous, just in case."

"Understood." I'm only sometimes the senior partner; it was Zev's recon, and that put him in tactical charge. Maybe nothing would happen other than they'd go out in the city and see both what they could find out and what kind of armament they could buy.

And in any case, it was pointless to give orders that would be obeyed or ignored as the situation warranted.

I'd have to slip away from the reception early, but that would likely not be a problem.

"Later, then. Be careful."

Zev's "Yes, sir," was scornful.

I walked them to the lift.

Alon had finished the inspection of the half-dozen officers on his side of the room, and walked over to me.

Some men were made to wear mess dress; some aren't. Even careful tailoring couldn't hide the fact that Alon was a few years past his prime, a few pounds overweight.

He hitched at his sword belt as he addressed the officers.

"To begin," he said. "The port manager's reception for the Casas and Freiheimers is a different kind of battlefield than most of you are used to. I don't want to arrive *en masse*, looking like an assault team, so we're going to go down at ten-minute intervals. You find the host, introduce yourself, then introduce yourself to the Casas and the Freiheimers, then mingle." He cracked a smile. "It's a good idea to start off the negotiations with a little theater. We're going to do that by building up to my arrival, with Gevat and Galil at each side, playing bodyguard."

He sighed. "It's all bullshit, of course, but the image is important. Now, orders: I want you all to remember that you are to talk as much as you must, and say as little as you need to. Basically, all we're doing is showing the flag. The real negotiating will happen between me and Giacometti on the Casa side, and me and Holtenbrenner on the Freiheim side.

"So just enjoy yourselves, stay out of fights, drink less than you eat, keep your ears open. You want to add anything to that, Inspector-General?"

I shook my head. I could have added something about how operations officers always tend to overplan everything, even after they've become generals, but that didn't seem politic. "Nothing much. There will likely be some representatives of private mercenary companies there. They should know enough to keep their distance, but if not, the peacemakers will keep things calm and orderly. Don't go looking for trouble."

I have this theory about foreign cultures, involving beautiful women and public places. It goes like this: the number of beautiful women in public places is in inverse relation to both the inherent desirability of the women involved and the gradient of wealth to poverty in that society.

Put more simply, beautiful women have something they can trade for not having to go out and be jostled by the dirty, poor, and ugly.

The richer the rich are, compared with the poor, the more impetus the poor have to trade it in.

The sharper the difference between the wealthy and the poor in any society, the more motivation lower-class girls have for finding a man of a higher class to take them away from it all, no matter what he wants in return; the sharper the motivation for middle-class women to do anything rather than fall to the bottom.

A quick eyeball estimate suggested that, of the thousand or so people at the manager's reception, fully ten percent were lovely women. Yet another point for my theory.

Clinging to the arm of a fat man in an elegant purple knee-coat and silken breeches, a long-haired redhead smiled an invitation at me. She wore a clinging silver sequined dress that must have cost her mackereau plenty. It was gathered at the neck, and slit in the front to an impressive cleavage, and slit up almost to her left hip on the side. She gave a half-turn away, letting me see that her dress left her back bare from the neck almost to the base of the spine.

I returned the smile for just a moment, until she turned back to her companion and gave a deep-throated, totally sympathetic laugh at whatever he'd just said.

I know what the laugh of a whore sounds like. I left the laugh behind.

The first step was to find the host.

I found Port Manager Bercuson at the far end of the room, an overweight, over-jeweled dowager, presumably his wife, at his side. They were engaged in conversation with a dozen men and women in TW Commerce Department formal finery: high-collared black suits, brass buttons down the front, black trousers with gold stripes on the men, knee-length pleated black skirts on the women, rank insignia on collars and sleeves, medals and ribbons on the left breast.

He carried more hardware than any of the others: the four broad stripes on his sleeve, proclaiming him a manager, got him off to a good start.

I've never quite figured out what the Commerce Department gives its people medals for, and I've never really bothered to ask. It's more fun guessing, and I've made up my private translation table. He had the Loss of Baggage Cross with three oak leaf clusters as the senior medal, accompanied by a Dithering Device, a Prolonged Negotiation Cross, and two of the strange little devices that really look like golden nails, as in "for want of a nail . . ."

"Good evening, Manager Bercuson."

I didn't have a nameplate on the left side of my tunic, but he had apparently been briefed.

"Inspector-General Tetsuo Hanavi." His handshake was moist, but correct. "I'm so pleased that you could join us this evening." He indicated the woman on his right. "My wife, Elena. Dear, this is the inspector-general I was telling you about. He's going to make sure that Metzada fulfills its contract to whichever side they sign on with in the upcoming Nueva war."

Unusual. Usually CD people try to pretend that all wars are avoidable, if only the right words are said at the right time.

She gave a half-sniff. At that, the conversation around us quickly died off.

Don't worry about it, old woman. I bathed fairly recently.

I had to throw something into the silence. "Very kind of you to give this reception, Manager," I said.

His smile may have been genuine. "Not at all, Inspector-General, not at all. Most of the Thellonee's trade is half the continent away at Mukachevo these days; any excuse for a reception is a pleasure. Which isn't to say," he quickly added, "that your being here is any less of an honor."

Or any more of one, either.

I stayed another couple of minutes, until the conversation overloaded my banality circuits, then made my excuses and left.

Over by the east wall, under a Boccaccio tapestry of nymphs and satyrs frolicking in a wooded glen, the Casalingpaesan general was holding court, several dozen officers and companions waiting on his words with either bated breath or a politic simulation.

I hitched at my swords and made my way over towards the Casas. A much-beribboned, fortyish colonel of artillery nodded a greeting, and opened his mouth to say something when the general stopped what he was saying and turned to me.

"Tetsuo Hanavi," General Vittorio Giacometti exclaimed, with what sounded like genuine pleasure. "How long has it been?"

He was an unabashedly portly man, the scarlet tunic and glistening black trousers of his uniform perfectly tailored. Handing his glass to his companion, a slim, dark-haired girl who couldn't have been more than eighteen, he walked over and gripped my shoulders. "And with stars on your shoulders, yet. Well done, boy, well done. How long has it been?"

"A few years, General," I said. "I think it was that time outside of Anchorville?"

I knew it was that time outside of Anchorville, and he knew it was that time outside Anchorville, but maybe there was somebody who didn't listening in.

"Ahh . . . Correggio it's now called. Yesyesyes," he said. "You don't look any older, though that was ten years or so ago." He turned to the civilian at his right, a fiftyish, square-jawed Casa who looked almost too neat and clean in his black kneecoat and breeches, like he'd just been unwrapped from the plastic.

"Almost eleven," I said. "I had some difficulty on Rand a couple years back. My face had to be rebuilt a little."

One of his officers, a major whose face was heavily firescarred, looked at me long and steadily. I couldn't tell if he was glaring at me; his face was the rigid, expressionless mask that fire leaves behind.

Sorry, Major. If Casalingpaesa wants to pay for Metzadan reconstructive surgery, they're welcome to. It's not cheap. But we don't export that kind of information. Generally, you can only sell information once, and not for enough.

Giacometti cleared his throat. "In any case . . . Ambassador Gianpaulo Adazzi, Inspector-General Tetsuo Hanavi," he said, presenting me with an elegant flourish.

I bowed, not deeply. "Ambassador."

"Inspector-General."

"The ambassador is my superior, General. He'll be doing the

negotiating for Casalingpaesa. We are big on civilian control, you know."

I was surprised, but it wouldn't do to act surprised. "I know about civilian control," I said, taking a light tone. "It's one of the perversions you offworlders fall subject to," I added with a smile.

Giacometti turned to snap his fingers at the crowd of officers and companions at his left. "Are there no manners here?" the general said. "One of you run to the bar and get a drink for the Inspector-General—and quickly, quickly, quickly, before he dies of thirst. Whiskey, General?"

"Scots whiskey, if they have it." Another guilty pleasure. It's remarkable how much soup could be made with the barley that goes into just one liter of whiskey.

"Wonderful exercise, Correggio was," Giacometti went on. "One of your brother's early commands, as I recall."

"One of them." His first, really, but that wasn't how Ari had been advertised.

Reclaiming his glass, the general took a quick slurp before addressing the assemblage. "Simply wonderful. His brother found a unique way of motivating a tired unit. Absolutely saved the day. Absolutely." He waited, expectantly.

One of the captains took the bait. "Unique way, General?"

"Yes," Giacometti said, with a smile. "He called in an enemy artillery barrage on his own position. It worked beautifully."

That wasn't quite how it happened, but it was close enough.

"It did, at that," I said, proud that there was not even a trace of irony in my voice.

Despite the almost clownish demeanor, it would have been a mistake to underrate Giacometti. His chest was covered with medals—which wouldn't necessarily mean much; a Casa private usually carries almost enough brass on his chest to make a cannon—but just under the senior Casa decoration was the Two Swords, with Shimon's three unauthorized red stitches. Vittorio Giacometti was one of Shimon Bar-El's cronies, from the first time Shimon was on Nueva.

My uncle never picks his people haphazardly.

A baby-faced lieutenant arrived with a glass and an apologetic grimace. "I hope this is satisfactory, General. Glenforres, it's called. The bartender says that's the only Scots whiskey he has."

"Fine." I accepted the glass. Any one would have been fine; it's hard to develop a discriminating palate for whiskies when you have your first taste at sixteen, and that only the harsh stuff we use at home for the Mercenary's Toast.

The ambassador ignored Giacometti's attempt to change the subject. "You don't approve of civilian control, then. May one inquire as to why?"

"Nothing personal, Ambassador. It's just that civilians tend to keep modifying objectives and making tactical and strategic decisions they've got no business making. Instructions from civilians to the military should consist of one word: win."

"Very interesting. And one should leave to the military the question of what is a 'win' and what means to do it with?"

"Not necessarily." I sipped at my whiskey. "Only if you've got the right military. They can do better with what you have than you think they can." I smiled genially at him. "End of free lesson. The next one costs."

He took a moment to think that over. "I've decided that wasn't intended as an insult. Why am I right?"

I decided that I liked this ambassador. "Because we're always professionals, and you aren't. You've got some fine officers, in and out of uniform. Ditto for the best of your NCOs.

"But you don't have any blooded privates, damned few good NCOs left in the companies, and what blooded company-grade officers you have are the losers who haven't even been able to make major in ten years of peace. That leaves you vulnerable in a way that the Freiheimers aren't: they've got a stronger martial tradition than you have. You've lost too many good men to civvy street, and promoted too many good paper-pushers in the past ten years."

I turned to Giacometti. "Present company excepted, General," I said levelly, hoping that he understood that I wasn't speaking just out of politeness. Giacometti may have seemed half-clown in a social setting, but I'd seen him run a division.

"So why Metzada? Why not some of the private companies?" Adazzi asked.

I shrugged. "That's the kind of question you should be saving for General Alon, and his staff. I'm just the IG. He can tell you what the private companies are capable of, individually and collectively. Forgetting for the moment that none of them can put together anything larger than a beefed-up regiment, we're better. Not cheaper. Better." I smiled. "Meaner."

"That may well be," Adazzi said, his voice holding only a trace of the skepticism he wanted me to know he felt.

"Ladies and gentlemen, a toast," the general said. "To renewed acquaintances."

"Renewed acquaintances." I drained the glass.

"Speaking of your brother, is he among your party, by any chance?" Giacometti asked.

"Sorry, no—his battalion just got home from Thuringia. He's taking some well-earned rest with his family."

"Ahh. Unfortunate. One of our party was his exec, in his old company. Major Paulo Stuarti? You recall?"

I nodded; I recalled. A good hand with a handgun, even if he was a bit too quick with the hip flask. Although . . . just a major? Unless his performance had degraded one hell of a lot over the past decade, Stuarti should have been at least a light colonel. He was a damn fine combat officer.

I flagged a passing waiter, and snagged a couple of hors d'oeuvres from his silver tray.

"I don't see him." I wasn't sure what it was on the crackers, but it tasted agreeably salty.

"He is somewhere around; it's far too early for him and his companion to have retired. There was somebody else here, wanting to meet you—an assistant police prefect, something-or-other Dunnigan? Dunfey, I think it is. Yes, yes, Dunfey. You should keep an eye out for him." The tone was a dismissal.

"That I should." Probably the usual don't-get-into-trouble

warning, which I'd best put off as long as possible. I nodded, again. "Good to see you again, sir."

"Be well, Inspector-General. Be well."

Leaving the empty glass on a table, I worked my way through the crowd toward the other side of the room. Both etiquette and common sense would keep Casalingpaesans and Freiheimers on opposite sides of the room, and I'd have to seem to pay equal attention to both. Giacometti was fully capable of finesse; it was possible that he really didn't want me to spend more than a few minutes with his opposite number. Or maybe he didn't want me to irritate the ambassador too much.

I was almost all the way across the room when she caught my arm.

It's one move to turn, block and strike, but there are thousands of combinations.

I turned slowly and smiled.

"How are you this evening?" she asked, her even smile more promise than invitation. Again, she tossed her head to give me the effect of her long red hair spilling down her mostly-naked back. I was grateful, of course, but didn't know quite how to thank her.

"Fine. And how have you been?"

"Oh? Have we met before?"

"Pardon my bluntness." Or don't. I've met you on a dozen worlds, lady. "But who are you?"

"Well," she said, tucking her hand under my arm, "you can call me Melanie. And I'm more of a what than a who."

"Really? Then what are you?"

"I'm sort of your present for tonight. With General Giacometti's compliments." She said the words easily, without embarrassment, as though being a whore were a simple fact, like the sun rising in the morning.

This was surprising. Giacometti should have known better than to try and bribe me. Not that I wouldn't take a bribe, mind; that's permitted. Doing something you weren't otherwise going to do in return for a bribe is what is forbidden. Strictly.

"I have to pay my respects to the Freiheimers," I said.

"They are this way," she said, pulling gently on my arm.

You can't serve under Shimon Bar-El without something of him rubbing off on you. My brother learned command presence; I picked up something else.

General Manfred Holtenbrenner made me want to reach for my swords.

He was a tall man, even taller than I am, his back ramrod straight, his black Freiheimer uniform elegantly edged in gold. Almost all of him was studiously elegant. His hair was black, carefully flecked with gray only at the temples. A slim tabstick dangled from his lower lip; he reached up incongruously stubby fingers to take it out as he greeted us.

To his right, a watery-eyed, blond lieutenant wearing an aide's golden aiguillette watched me carefully, as though there were something the pasty-faced little bastard could do if I decided I wanted the general dead. I returned his level, almost frankly hostile gaze with a weak smile, resisting the urge to let some threat shine through.

After all, the IG is a noncombatant.

"Guten abend, Herr General," I said.

He waved it away. "English, please, Inspector-General," he said in a voice that held no accent, except, perhaps, a bit of extra guttural on the voiced consonants.

"Tetsuo Hanavi," I said.

"I am Manfred Holtenbrenner," he gave more of a medium nod than a slight bow, but not much more. "And the young lady?"

Perhaps there was a trace of a sneer on his lip, just a bit of knowing scorn in his voice; perhaps not. But I remembered—

Shimon Bar-El's face is greasy in the firelight. "Frei-heimers, they call themselves," he says. "Freiheimers. I remember them. I remember Amalek," he says. There is a small leather-covered Bible in his left hand, but he's not reading from it. He doesn't have to, not for these verses.

"Then came Amalek, and fought with Israel in Riphidim.

"And Moshe said to Yehoshua: 'Choose men, and go out and fight with Amalek; tomorrow I will stand on the top of the hill with the rod of the Lord in my hand.'

"Yehoshua did as Moshe said to him, and fought with Amalek; and Moshe, Aaron, and Hur went up to the top of the hill. And it came to pass, when Moshe held up his hand, that Israel prevailed, and when he let down his hand, Amalek prevailed.

"But Moshe's hands were heavy, so they took a stone and put it under him, and he sat on it. And Aaron and Hur held up his hands, one on one side, one on the other, and his hands were steady until the sun went down.

"And Yehoshua discomfitted Amalek and his people with the edge of the sword.

"And the Lord said to Moshe, 'Write this for a memorial in the book, and rehearse it in the ears of Yehoshua, for I—I, Shimon Bar-El—will utterly blot out the remembrance of Amalek from under heaven.' And Moshe built an altar, and called it The Lord Is My Banner, and he said, 'With my hand on the throne of the Lord, I swear that the Lord will have war with Amalek from generation to generation.'"

He tucks the Bible back in his khaki shirt and makes us all wait while he buttons his shirt carefully over it.

"I remember," he says, his voice a quiet murmur, almost a whisper. We all have to hold our breath to hear him now, and that's probably just the way he wants it. "I remember Amalek. Let the rest of the universe forget, I remember. You think Amalek perished there, in Riphidim?

"No. I say to you that Amalek is here, and I tell you that I have a war to finish with Amalek." Tears stream

down his broad face; he seems to stagger for a moment,
then he recovers.

"More." He holds up his hands as he looks me square
in the face. Me, out of the hundreds there. "I tell you
that you have a war with Amalek. And here is where
you face him—"

I looked him square in the face. My brother was right:
Shimon would not have passed us knowledge that we could
use to strike a deal with Freiheim. I didn't see all the traps,
but it didn't matter. If we were to get involved in the war, it
would be alongside the Casas again.

It had long been decided, maybe even in Riphidim.

Knowing that felt good, but it didn't matter how I felt about
it. It wasn't my decision. It was the old man's. Again. I felt
distant, as though all this were happening a long way away,
my mouth and limbs controlled by a distant puppeteer. But I
was, at that moment, unable to resent it, any more than the
puppet does.

"The young lady," I heard myself saying, "is a whore, of
good Junker stock, that my friend General Giacometti is giving
me for the night."

The temperature dropped about twenty degrees. Melanie's
grip tightened on my arm, and her smile froze.

I didn't move. Over by the nearest door, two of the peacemakers in their formal uniforms turned toward us, hands
resting near the butts of their wireguns. Just as my swords are
part of my dress uniform, so are their guns.

I smiled at the general. *If it happens, you're first.* Then the
aide.

For a moment, I honestly didn't know which way it would
go, but then Holtenbrenner threw back his head and laughed.
It sounded hollow to me, but it was enough for the claque of
listeners around him. They joined in, one of the women with a
nervous titter that earned her a glare from the watery-eyed
blond aide.

"A strong joke, my dear Inspector-General. We're all fortunate that I prize myself on my sense of humor, and my open-mindedness. Besides, your lovely companion is a red-head—of a different branch of our Aryan race entirely."

For a few moments we made polite conversation, words passing lips almost mechanically, until I could find a way to leave.

I turned and walked away, Melanie on my arm. Damn me, but it had felt good to taunt the German.

Freiheimer, Freiheimer.

"What now?" she said, a trace of a quaver in her voice.

"Now you earn your money."

I led her toward the doors that led to the lifts. The first car that came was empty.

"Can I ask what that was all about?" she said, after the lift doors closed and I thumbed for my rooms in the penthouse.

As the car accelerated, I stooped to retrieve a pair of tabsticks from my sock, thumbed them both to life, and passed her one. "Just a guilty pleasure," I said.

The door hissed open in my rooms.

As she took the tabstick away from her lips, I put my free arm around her and pulled her close. With a practiced one-handed gesture, she reached a slim hand up to the back of her neck. Her dress dropped to the floor. Beneath it, she was naked and lovely.

CHAPTER
EIGHT Night Moves

Thellonee, New Britain
New Portsmouth Port Facility
01/10/44, 2327 local time

"Wha' is i'?" Melanie said, her voice muffled by the pillow.

"Just me," I said, as I came out of the bathroom with the hypo loaded and ready. I thought she was going to stay face down on the pillow, but she turned over and her eyes widened. She was too slow; I whipped the sheets away and batted her hands aside as I pressed its snout to her shoulder. It hissed briefly.

I let her go, backed away and watched her eyes glaze over before they sagged shut. I picked up her wrist and timed her pulse with my thumbnail watch. Fifty beats per minute.

I allowed myself a smile as I let her arm drop. I retrieved a bottle of the local vodka from the top of the dresser, carefully rinsing her mouth out with about an ounce of the stuff, letting it slosh onto the pillow; I didn't want her inhaling it.

Not only would the drug keep her unconscious until morning, but it wiped out short-term memory, the same way a just-this-side-of-lethal overdose of alcohol does. She'd wake up with a horrible hangover and a bruise on her arm. Not really unusual for a whore.

She was a question mark, and while that hadn't deterred me from bedding her, I wasn't going to push my luck. A few centiliters of clear liquid and she was an ellipsis. She was probably just what she seemed to be, but so what? Whatever she was wouldn't be a problem for at least eight hours. I would, I hoped, be back at the hotel well before then, and actually sleeping with strange women isn't one of my guilty pleasures.

Well, one of us has to move, and it might as well be me, I thought. I pulled on a robe, packed up my gear and moved it into one of the penthouse's empty bedrooms, then registered the change with the hotel's computer.

On my last trip, I looked at her lying on the bed, hair spilling over the pillow. She looked kind of sweet and kind of vulnerable there, and I caught myself wondering about what kind of life she lived, and what kind of life she was going to live, until I decided that it really wasn't any of my business, and closed the door behind me.

I never saw her again.

Closing the door behind me in my new room, I dropped the robe to the floor and shrugged into my clothes, a gray gripsuit and a brown trailcoat, then sat to pull on my jump boots. There's a lot to be said for the traditional slippers, but one of the nice things about jump boots is that they give great support to your ankles, handy if you're going to fall any distance.

I was about to leave when the light began flashing on the message board by the door.

Please call me at your earliest convenience at PREFECT–2, the message said. *Nigel Dunfey, AsstPrefect, New Portsmouth Constabulary.*

I didn't like it. Doctrine is to stay away from local police. What did this one want? It couldn't be related to Zev and Dov; he had apparently been looking for me at the party, before they left. Odds were he wanted to warn me off of something, and the longer I could operate without confronting the local authorities, the better.

The Sergeant was waiting for me in the living room, the others having gone to bed. Like me, he was dressed for the outside, except that his gripsuit was almost comically tight across his middle. "You're not going alone," he said.

"Sure I am," I said. "I don't need you yet. Not for this."

He couldn't leave it at that. "What's the real reason?"

I lit a tabstick and returned his look. "Because you can't jog ten klicks anymore, much less run for ten, and because I don't want to play Samson-in-the-temple. We don't walk through trouble, not yet. We run away. You can't do that, old man."

He looked at me, thinking it over.

There are worlds where a sergeant, no matter how experienced and salty, when told to do something by his commanding general, just goes ahead does it. Give me an army of men like the Sergeant and I'll leave any of those worlds aflame from pole to pole.

"Four hours," he said. "And you'll stay out of trouble."

"Four hours," I said.

I slipped out a side door and into the rain, walking briskly down the side of the road for the Preserve gate, a little more than a klick away.

Traffic was light at that hour; only a pair of lorries hissed by me, heading outward, the spray from their skirts sending me huddling in my trailcoat.

I nodded at the camera as the fence clanked aside, then stepped out into the street. Security is only tight when entering the Preserve, not leaving it.

The nearest mono station was just a block away. When I climbed the rickety wooden steps to the more solid concrete platform, Zev and Dov were already there, as was an old couple who huddled with their packages in the far corner of the filthy shack, clearly terrified of us, equally terrified that any demonstration of their fear would only set us off. The unblinking red eye of the shack's security camera didn't seem to reassure them.

I wondered what they were doing out this late, but couldn't think of a good reason to ask.

The mono's flat rail curved off into the distance, hanging above most of the city, dividing it horizontally as well as vertically. Above, in the high-rising buildings toward the core of the city, life was safe and warm. Below, the day belonged to the workers, protected, sometimes, if they were lucky, by the prowl cars of the Constabulary.

In the distance a light flickered on the rail; a train of three sleek cars, their sides glistening with wetness, slowed and then stopped. The elderly couple got on.

"This ours?" I asked.

Zev shook his head. "We need an odd-numbered train." As the door hissed shut and the train pulled away from the station, he turned his back to the camera.

"Not a lot to report," he said. "There's crime, but it's hard to get anyone to talk about who's doing what to who, and for how much. Some drug trade from the west—all flavors of alkaloids, mainly. Around the core towers, you can find a whole assortment of sex partners, but I don't see anything useful there. Gang action in the core city and out in Somerset: some of the young turks are taking territory away from the old-line New Portsmouth transportee types, but mainly from each other. Political corruption all over the place; the new mayor is promising to clean up the Constabulary, once and for all."

That didn't mean much to me.

"Anything to add to the G2 briefing?" I lit a tabstick and considered the coal's glow.

He shrugged. "Give me two years, and I'll give you a full report. You're expecting this to be too easy, I think."

Maybe I was. Maybe not. "I know Shimon Bar-El. If he wants to be found, he'll be findable."

Dov hadn't said a word, but at this he nodded.

"So what? If we do find him, is it worth it?" Zev shrugged. "What's he going to do for us that's so important?"

I didn't answer; I didn't know. But the Intelligence reports said that Shimon was involved somehow with local criminal activity. Since we didn't have forever to try to find him, the only thing to do was to make contact with as many different criminal individuals and organizations as we could, and hope to find something that would lead us to him. The young hoodlums weren't the most promising place to start, but they were easy—we could approach them directly tonight, and then see what we could do with drug dealers and pimps tomorrow.

Another car hissed its way into the station. This one had a flashing green "3" on its side. Above the door, under the flaking painted letters that said NEXT STOP, the sign changed from PRESERVE to 39TH AND 4TH.

New Portsmouth is well designed. I've been in cities where they name streets—and not alphabetically, just give them whatever name is handy.

"Here we go," Zev said, pulling a flimsy from his pocket as we stepped aboard. The car was empty. "Any three, five, or nine will bring you back, eventually—but take the express, if possible." The doors hissed shut behind us. Smoothly, the train pulled away from the station.

"We going anywhere in particular?"

"Yes, but . . . no promises any good'll come of it." Zev shrugged. "There may be some action over in Somerset, by the Common. I have a meeting set up at a bar called The Dangling Prussian."

"Oh?" I smiled; that sounded like the kind of place that Shimon would be involved with.

Zev had picked up on that. "I doubt it, but I guess it's possible. The name isn't new; it was here last time I was. We're arms smugglers—we've gotten or are about to get a shipload of slugthrowers past Customs. I wasn't too explicit."

A reasonable cover. In places where the manufacture or import of guns are forbidden or strictly controlled, you can always get a lot of interest from people on the other side of the law in illicit weapons. "Why not wireguns, instead?"

He snickered. "We didn't have a demo wiregun."

Dov patted at his chest.

Very nice, indeed. "How long to Somerset?"

He glanced down at his thumbnail. "Twenty minutes. And then a short walk. The bar's near the station. It's under the rail."

They were younger than I'd expected. The youngest was maybe thirteen, the oldest perhaps seventeen. There were six of them, dressed in brown trousers and white pullover shirts, with few places bare of grease or filth. Three of them crammed into the bench opposite Zev and me, while the other three took up an almost-military at-rest position near Dov, who was leaning against the flaking wall.

Dov didn't say anything. He's fluent in several languages, but he can't drop the Metzadan burr from his voice. It takes practice, and that's not something he practices. Shimon never told him to.

"Names first," the leader said. "I'm Davy. This is Ilene, and Arthur. The three fellows standing opposite your boy are Kurt, Bradley, and Eric. You are?"

Why I'm Tetsuo Havani, inspector-general, Metzada. Have you seen my uncle recently? "I'm Mr. Brown. He's Mr. Black," I said, indicating Zev.

Davy snickered. "And the ox?"

"He's Mr. Large," I said.

He spent a solid second deciding how to handle it, and then chose a laugh. Good choice.

"Names don't matter," I said. "I wouldn't give you a real one, or tell you anything you could go to the Constabulary with, so why bother with names? All you care about is my merchandise, so Mr. Black tells me. All I care about is what kind of money you have."

"Let's see it," said the fat boy, Arthur. "I want to see it."

His nose had been broken in too many fights, and his left ear looked like somebody had once let his dog teethe on it, if there were dogs on Thellonee.

"Patience," Zev said. "Wait for the drinks."

It had been a neighborhood bar, once. Long ago, Somerset had been the outskirts of New Portsmouth, but as the inner part of the city had decayed, business had moved east, to Somerset.

You don't cure a disease by moving away from it. Now Somerset was the inner-city itself: hard-bitten, filthy. Out on the street, past the dirty glasses stacked at the far end of the bar, past the dirty glass of the window, there were more of them waiting for us. Just in case things didn't work out in here.

Guns might be at a premium in New Portsmouth, but wherever there's steel, there are knives.

The bartender, a round-shouldered man of about fifty, arrived with our tray of beer in unopened brown glass bottles. He set the tray down, and debated with himself for a moment whether or not to try to collect now.

"On me," I said, slowly bringing my hands out of my coat with a five in my left hand, three ones in my right. It's not a good idea to flash a roll; much better to keep all your fives in one pocket, your ones in another. That way, you can produce what you need—without letting anyone know what you have.

The bartender scampered away with his money. But he kept eyeing the phone behind the bar, although he was too smart to pick it up. It might have taken less than a minute for the Prefecture to get a floater to the bar, but—assuming that the young lads wouldn't cut him to ribbons in that minute—he still had to live in this neighborhood.

Davy was maybe fifteen. Not the oldest one in the group, but he seemed to have the cleverest eyes. "How many can you supply? And when? Tonight?"

"No." I shook my head. "It'll be a few days, maybe a week." If we couldn't find Shimon Bar-El in a week, we couldn't find him at all. Besides, the negotiating team was only going to be here for a week. "And the question isn't how many we can supply—it's how many you can afford. Guns are expensive. Only a few this trip. More next." That would appeal to him; if we were able to supply him with enough weaponry to give his gang an ascendancy over the other ones, he'd be able to recruit even more members.

"At least twenty, I need at least twenty," he said, flatly. "I can give you a thousand each, for twenty."

I snickered. "A thousand? Local pounds or TW chits?"

"Local money. Where are we going to get tweeks?"

"Your problem." I made as though to rise. "If you can't come up with better than that, we won't do business here at all—I can have the stuff come in at another port." I eyed him steadily. "If we can't do business, I'll be out of the city tomorrow, and I won't be back."

He nodded his appreciation that I had worked that one out, saving him the trouble of explaining that if I wasn't going to deal with the Storm, I wasn't going to deal with any of the other gangs in New Portsmouth. One way or the other, I wasn't going to deal with the competition. Possibly a price would go on my head the instant negotiations fell through; more likely they'd just pull out their knives.

"I'll make it fifteen hundred," he said. "We need some weapons."

So I understood. The gang wars were heating up throughout New Portsmouth. The high scores seemed to be being run up by a gang called the Vators.

Sitting next to him was a greasy-haired girl of perhaps sixteen. She eyed me unblinkingly, her expression blank, then turned to look out the window.

"Constabs," she said.

"Shit," the leader said. "Nige, scramble—and watch it. Move out in groups. Shaveteeth prolly called in the 'stabs; could be waiting to jump solos."

The tall boy ran for the front door and started calling out orders.

"I don't hear—" Zev began.

"Listen. Five nights from now," he said, looking at me. "Seventh and Twenty-Ninth, near the port." They were already crowding out of the booth; so was Zev.

By the time we were all on our feet, a constabulary floater, red lights flashing and siren moaning, had tilted itself to a stop in front of the bar, and uniformed proctors in riot gear were sending sparks off into the night as their wands slashed at the retreating young gangsters.

Davy headed for the back door, his companions in full pursuit. We followed them. It occurred to me that if the local police were really interested in rounding up the gangs, they'd watch all the doors, possibly with the main force at the rear door, the floater acting as a beater.

We ducked out the back door and into a cobblestoned alley that was empty of everything except dirt and garbage. A hundred feet above our heads, a train hummed by, shaking water from its sides in a momentary torrent as it banked into a turn.

Davy and his five young toughs scrambled up the fire escape.

"Do we follow them?"

I shook my head. We could better explain being found in a back alley than creeping around rooftops.

Me in the lead, the three of us went to the end of the alley and peered out. Nothing. Behind us, we could hear the distant moan of the police siren and the shrill screams of the young toughs touched by the police wands, but there was nothing here.

We slipped off into the night and worked our way back to the next mono stop, and took the train back to the hotel.

Corporal Menachem Yabotinsky was waiting in the living room when the three of us came in, dripping water on the rug. Without being asked, he poured three glasses of whiskey and passed them around, then sat down and rubbed tired hands across his face. He looked at least ten years older than his fifty-or-so.

I took a long pull on the drink. "Long night?"

"Nah." He shrugged it off, then scratched at his almost hairless head. "I just got on. The ham is good, but the chicken is horrible, just like mother used to make." He gestured to the tray of coffee and sandwiches on the dining table. "I've stood watch under worse conditions, although usually with a bit more armament." He had a makeshift spear leaning against the wall: a Fairbairn knife duct-taped tightly to a two-meter length of aluminum pipe.

"Where'd you get the pipe?"

"Basement." He shrugged. "They've got some extra plumbing stock. Didn't figure they'd miss it."

Zev snickered as he drained his whiskey, then poured himself another one. "You figure to need a spear here?"

Yabotinsky shook his head. "Nah. Probably not. Never in my life needed a weapon, unless I needed one real bad."

Dov spoke up. "I'll lend you my pistol until morning, Corporal, if you want me to."

"Pistol? Yeah, I wouldn't mind borrowing a pistol."

At Yabotinsky's nod, Dov produced his Korriphila, and handed it to the smaller man. Yabotinsky quickly field-stripped it, then reassembled it.

"Nice," he said, setting the pistol on the table in front of him. "I'll take good care of it."

"You haven't asked whether we found him yet or not," Zev said.

"I figured you haven't, or you might have mentioned it." The corporal shrugged. "Doesn't make a whole lot of difference to me. I'm not a planner; never have been. None of us are. Don't ask us for clever plans. Clever plans are for the folks with bars, leaves, or stars on their shoulders, not stripes on their sleeves. You do the planning, show us who and tell us when, then stand the fuck out of our way."

CHAPTER NINE Diane Emmett & Son

Morning coffee in front of us, tabsticks burning in ashtrays, Zev and I were going over a map of the city, trying to sort out the day's activities when Alon walked into the living room, alone.

"Tetsuo," he said. "I want to pick your brains."

Zev scowled at that, as though we had any choice about whether or not to consult with DCSOPS Alon.

"Yes, David?" He may have ranked me, but we both wore a star on each shoulder. I gestured him to a chair and pushed my pack over to him. He nervously pulled one out and fired it up, washing down the smoke with a swig of coffee from Zev's cup—before he realized what he was doing and set it down.

"Sorry, Zev. Tetsuo, we're having a bit of a problem. And not just with the Freiheimers." He gave me a long glare at that point, and when I didn't react, he just shrugged and went on. "I'm meeting a bit of resistance from the Casa ambassador. It's the usual why-pay-premium-prices argument, but I think he may not be listening to my answer."

There's only one answer to that argument, and it's that you get what you pay for: generally speaking, mercenary outfits consist of scum soldiers, with little esprit de corps, no willingness to take heavy casualties whatever the need, and a lot less value than they appear to have, which isn't much. Further, mercenaries often have a temptation to rob the paymaster, instead of fighting for him. Metzada is different; if we start robbing any employers, future employers aren't going to be interested in us.

But if Adazzi wasn't listening to the answer, if he wasn't paying attention to what Giacometti—as well as Alon, presumably—was telling him, I didn't see what I could do.

I shrugged. "One of their party was the exec in my brother's company," I said. "You know, the Casas Shimon had put under Metzadan command. Good man. I can talk with him."

"Do that."

"I will. You've got to remember that he's working for Casalingpaesa, not us. Ari might be able to call in some personal loyalty, but nobody else. Not even Shimon, and not me. I didn't do much at all for him."

Actually, Paulo Stuarti and I had once killed a bunch of Casa Loyalty Detachment soldiers together, but they were going for their own weapons at the time. "But won't the Casas see some sort of side-discussion as an admission of . . ."

"Desperation?" He shook his head. "We're not desperate, no, not desperate, but we could easily use a good contract for an armored division, or even a reinforced RCT. Still . . . let it slide another day or so, and then give it a try. Subject to what you have to do on your own assignment. Any luck with that, yet?"

"Not yet. We'll see." I thought it over for a moment, and then nodded. "I'll talk to him, in a couple of days. Can't see any harm in it."

The rest of that day, and the next, and most of the next night, were more of the same. We met with hoodlums and pimps, dealers in drugs and weapons, and others.

I spent a sweaty few minutes in a tall office building with a short, fat man who never turned from the window while we spoke. His three stocky bodyguards kept an eye on me, the two nearest unarmed and nervous, the one halfway across the room holding a pistol that he never quite pointed in my direction.

I listened while he told me that he got either a piece of the profits from any illicit sales in New Portsmouth, or some pieces of the profiteer. I listened to him try a few variations on that theme while Dov waited in the outer office, wondering if he was going to have to come in after me. But Mr. O'Brien was sensible, and I was sensible, and his guards were sensible, and we smiled at each other over how awfully sensible we all were.

I walked out of the office with a dry mouth and damp armpits, and still with no idea of where in New Portsmouth Shimon Bar-El was.

I sent Dov on a mono tour of the city, not expecting much, except that he'd come back. He did, although without any information.

I brought up the city directory on the screen in the living room, and had the oldsters search for any anagram of Bar-El, or names like Barrel, or something, but they found nothing, Wherever Shimon was wasn't obvious. Or so it seemed.

Particularly at night, Vicar's Park wasn't my idea of a great place to meet someone. This time, I was waiting for the Street Demons, yet another one of the gangs—this one formed mainly of newbies of Irish extraction, living up near One Hundred Twenty-eighth and Twelfth in Little Dublin—but it was their idea, and it would have to do.

There were six of them, all street-tough, three of them carrying canes that they surely didn't need to help them walk, another sporting a length of chain that was wrapped around his waist as sort of a belt, the other two apparently unarmed.

Only apparently, I assumed. You can prevent factories from turning out guns and ammunition, but a foot-long bar of steel can be turned into a knife even if all you have is some concrete to rub it against. It may not be a custom-balanced Fairbairn like the knife I was carrying in my coat, but crude weapons kill perfectly well.

"Who are you?" asked one, a thin-lipped boy. He seemed to have a permanent sneer carved into his face. It wasn't the only thing carved into his face; someone had once, apparently, spent a bit of time whittling away at it.

"I'm the gun salesman," I said. "Call me Mr. Brown, like the coat. I hear you want to buy some merchandise."

"Possible," he said. "Definitely possible. Show me some samples, then we can talk price. Once we know how you're going to smuggle quantity in. Best we've heard of is a couple at a time. Good enough for the Vators, maybe, but not good enough for us."

Overhead, stars peeked through the cloud cover, winking down at us. I didn't get the joke, but stars and I don't communicate too well.

"Sorry," I said. "I don't carry a sample with me. Next time. Now, let's talk price."

They all relaxed at that, and I realized that they had decided to jump me if it turned out I was armed; they were still puzzling over whether or not to settle for a gun in the hand or try for the jackpot of a whole delivery. But it seemed they decided to let me walk if I were cautious enough not to bring a weapon to a solo rendezvous.

We spent a couple of minutes haggling over price, and over when and where I would let them try out the merchandise before buying, and then I shook hands with their leader.

Something flickered momentarily across his face, and at the moment he let go of my hand I should have known they were going to try for a safe profit, for whatever I had on me, and not worry about whether or not I could import guns and who I'd sell them to.

I should have known. I should have picked up some hints that their raggedness was more from poverty than choice—something, anything.

He was an experienced little knife-artist. His right hand

dipped down to his side, and came back up with his switch-blade. The blade clicked into place with a decided *snap.*

It moved quickly—

"Quickly: are you paying attention?" he asks.

"Yes, Adoni, always."

Slowly, he seats himself across from me on the surface-grass mat. "There is only one way to teach you to pay attention to your surroundings," old Yehuda says, as we sit opposite each other, him in his well-worn gi belted across the middle with a simple white belt, me in my new one, proudly belted with green.

I'm so proud of myself—fourteen and already a green belt. I don't know why old Yehuda has given up his black belt for the white one of a beginner, and I don't know how to ask him why.

"There is only one way," he says.

"And that is?"

I never see his hand as it snakes out and slaps me across the face.

I bring my hand up to my stinging cheek. "Why did you do that? You're supposed to warn me before we spar."

"True," he says, his face grave. "We're not sparring. We're teaching you to—"

Whack. Again he slaps me across the face. Harder, this time.

"—pay attention."

Zev Aroni, one of the boys seated across the circle, laughs, until another instructor hits him across the back of the head.

"What'd you do that for?" he whines.

"Because you weren't paying attention."

From that moment on, at any time of the day, from the moment we report to Section for our noon classes until we leave at 1900 for dinner, our teachers will jump out of anywhere, at any moment, and hit us.

For me, it doesn't stop until the day I return to my quarters, shut the door behind me, and block old Yehuda's blow as he leaps out of the closet. He has never struck me outside of class before; he will never again try to strike me other than when we spar.

Tears stream down the old one's face as he hugs me. "Tetsuki," he says, "are you paying attention?"

I am paying attention, Adoni, I thought as I stepped back and blocked—the wrist, not the knife. The weapon is an extension of the hand. Stop the hand, you stop the weapon.

My left hand swept in, up, and out in a roundhouse block, the outside of my hand striking hard against his wrist, knocking it away. The hand is an extension of the arm. Stop the arm, you stop the hand.

The arm is an extension of the mind. Stop the mind, you stop the arm. I gripped his sleeve and pulled him to me as I brought my right arm around, hitting him hard on the temple with the heel of my hand.

His knees went loose and he crumpled as the others approached, spreading out, waiting to rush me. After all, what was I, one unarmed man?

I picked up their leader by the hair and brought his head up to about the level of my belly while I reached inside my coat to pull out my Fairbairn knife. It was about a third of a meter long, tapering gently to almost a needle point, razor-sharp on both edges—more of a dagger than anything else.

"I am more brutal than you," I said, setting the point of my blade against the unconscious boy's throat, just over the carotid. "You run or you die."

It might work. They had seen brutality, they had committed brutality, they'd kicked an unconscious enemy to death, perhaps, but maybe they hadn't seen murder in cold blood before.

One of them took a step forward, so I slashed through the leader's throat and kicked him away, arterial blood fountaining, bathing my forearm in dark wetness before I could kick him away.

One of them shrieked, and another's eyes widened, yet another shouted a too-late "No, no, don't," and three of them ran, but that left two, one armed with a cane, the other with a length of chain.

It should have been easy; the chain could endanger his partner as much as it did me. But the fat one with the chain held back while the pock-faced, black-haired boy with the cane moved in, neither of them saying a word.

He held the cane in front of him like a sword, lunging tentatively. I kept my knife close in and looked for an opening.

The one with the chain rattled it to distract my attention, and when I showed that I knew that one by not reacting, he whirled it over his head for a moment, the chain doubled over. He released one end, more throwing it at me than spinning the end toward me.

As I ducked under his swing, the other one moved in, lunging in full extension with his cane, but I wasn't where he expected me to be: I was a few centimeters to the left, bringing my leg up in a roundhouse kick that sent his cane spinning away into the night and left him off-balance, staggering toward me. I took a precious half-second to slide the knife between two ribs, but he jerked spasmodically and twisted away, taking my knife with him.

It didn't matter. The fat boy was just to my right, bringing his chain back for another swing. It caught me once, hard, in the side, but then I caught it with my left hand, and yanked on it, pulling him to me, and smashed my elbow into his face once, twice, three times.

He dropped the chain and brought his hands up to the bloody pulp that was all that was left of his nose. I kicked him solidly in the knee, then twice in the head when he fell. I kicked hard, like I was trying to kick a soccer ball into the goal.

He lay still after that.

I stooped to retrieve my knife from the body of the boy with the cane, then cleaned it on his shirt. I used the other one's shirt to towel off what blood I could, but my coat was still too clearly stained. I stripped it off and rolled it up, hiding my bloody hand and my knife in it, then walked quickly away, pressing my arm against my ribs where the one with the chain had hit me. It was starting to ache, badly.

Dammit, you can get hurt doing this, I thought.

If you're not moving your lips, bravado is cheap.

When I got back to our suite, the Sergeant was waiting for me next to the lift.

"There's an assistant police prefect in the living room waiting—what is it?" he said, concerned, when he saw I was pressing at my side.

"A bit of a mess." It wasn't feeling any better. "The blood isn't mine, but I took a kick in the side. The prefect got a name?"

"Dunfey. He says he's been waiting for you to make contact with him." The Sergeant eased me down the hall and into my room, and helped me lie down on the bed before he thumbed the phone on, not bothering to pick up the receiver. The pain seemed to get worse when I lay down, and it hadn't been a joy to begin with.

"Imran," a voice answered.

"Tetsuo's hurt, probably a cracked rib. His room."

"Right away."

The Sergeant thumbed the phone off and helped me out of my coat. He had me halfway out of my gripsuit when Ephraim Imran arrived, his canvas medician's bag in one hand.

"Been a long time since I did this for real," he said. "Which one is the patient?"

"Kill the chatter," the Sergeant said. "He says the blood's not his, but check him out anyway."

"I always do, and I was just whistling in the dark, Tzvi, just whistling in the dark," he said as he quickly unrolled the bag. "I always like to keep talking; it keeps the patient's mind off the pain. Now go and do sergeant things, and leave me alone."

The Sergeant thought it over, nodded, and left.

Unrolled, the medician's kit was a canvas sheet about a meter square, with bottles and instruments inserted in cloth loops.

"We're probably not going to have to do anything intrusive, so there's no need to get fancy, at least not at first." He tore the wrapping off a paper towel and rubbed it over his already-clean hands, then my side. It was cool and wet; I flinched. "Easy there, Tetsuo. Just watch the ceiling or something. Nothing to worry about."

He selected an instrument, a smooth gunmetal box about the size of a pack of tabsticks, with a screen built into one side, then thumbed it on. The screen flickered.

He didn't ask where I'd been injured; the skin was already purple.

"This won't hurt," he said, running it across my side. "Just a few sound waves, and—there it is." He snorted. "Cracked your ninth rib, that's all I can see. All I'm going to see, for the next while, unless we get you to some soft-tissue scanning gear. Which won't be necessary, I think." He pulled out a hypo, adjusting the dosage with a practiced spin of its barrel. "You going to be doing anything active for the next couple of days?"

"I hope so. Right now, I don't want to look like I'm hurting. Just give me some valda oil, tape my ribs and help me into the shower, and then a fresh uniform. I've just killed a few locals; I'd rather look like I've been out for a constitutional."

"I'd advise against the valda oil. It won't prevent you from moving that rib around—all it'll do is make sure you're not in pain while you're making things worse. I'd rather you feel it if anything else starts hurting."

"Just do it."

"Everybody's in such a rush these days." He sighed as he switched hypos, then adjusted the new one and pressed it briefly to my side. "Just valda oil, and a few vitamins," he said, as he set it down, then picked up a shaver. "Rather shave it off now than tear it off when I change the tape."

Nigel Dunfey, assistant prefect, New Portsmouth Constabulary, was the man they were thinking of when they invented the word "dapper." He was a compact man, half a head shorter than average, wearing a brown single-breasted kneecoat and matching trousers, a white silk brocade shirt, and an expression of infinite patience as he sat in a chair by the window.

Zev sat across from him, Moshe Stern and the Sergeant over by the wet bar. As Dunfey rose from his chair and turned his back to him, Zev mouthed, *Dov is sleeping,* which was the right way to do it: it was possible that Dunfey knew Hebrew.

"Prefect Dunfey?" I said, taking his proffered hand. "Tetsuo Hanavi. Please, sit down. The Sergeant has been making you comfortable, I hope?"

"Very much so, Inspector-General." He picked up his cup. Tea, probably. I hate tea. "I hope you are enjoying your stay here."

It usually takes bureaucrats quite a while to work up to what they want to say, but I didn't particularly want the Sergeant and his oldsters hanging around while he did. Particularly Moshe Stern; he tended to twitch.

"Thank you, Sergeant Hanavi," I said. "You and the private can go." The Sergeant looked at Stern, then jerked his chin in the direction of the door. Stern thought it over for a moment as he poured himself another glass of whiskey, no ice, and then shrugged and followed.

"I've been enjoying myself quite a lot, Prefect. Now, to be blunt, what can I do for you?"

"Let us be blunt." He shook his head for a moment. "I really don't understand why you simply do not come out with it. I would have thought you would wish to make contact with me immediately upon arrival."

"And why is that?"

"Or, at least, with my office," he went on, "before you began your research. I am the assistant prefect charged with the handling of youth gangs."

Beyond him, Zev smiled at me. A familiar hand was at work here.

"I'm sorry," I said. "I wasn't briefed on that."

"Really." He decided that he didn't believe me, and then let the word hang in the air until he decided it would be impolite to let his skepticism show any further. "I must say that there has been far too little formal communication in this whole affair. Now, granted, we cannot make it public that Metzada is consulting on how to handle our youth gang difficulties—the voters would wonder why they're paying the Constabulary, after all—but I hardly think that this passing of messages through intermediaries is at all the proper way to let us know that you might be available. In any case, shall we talk about terms for your consultation first, or should we go into an overview of the situation?"

"Situation?" I asked.

"Yes, yes, yes," he said impatiently. "I mean, obviously we are going to have to put it down as a security consultation instead of going into detail, but I assure you that any reasonable invoice will be paid. You are the Tetsuo Hanavi who is the expert on urban gang warfare, are you not?"

Well, as of now I was. "Who else would I be?" I steepled my hands in front of my face. "But before we go any further, I think I'd like a full briefing from you as to the situation."

"Well," he said, with a half-snort, "of course." He pulled his briefcase to his lap and pulled out a pile of flimsies, easily two thousand pages thick. He set the stack down on the table, and rose. "Will two days be long enough to go over it?"

It had better be, I thought. Alor's negotiators were due to wrap up their discussions in two days, and we were going to be homeward-bound then, if at all possible.

"Certainly," I said. "I'll have a bill drawn up by then. You'll have our recommendations and an estimate for contract police services in another month. And I can have some rough recommendations ready then."

"Really," he said, impressed. "You clearly have been doing some research. Thank you for seeing me, Inspector-General. I shall call on you in forty-eight hours. You have my phone code in case you need anything before then?"

"I do."

By the time he was out the door, I'd divided the sheaf into sections, and was passing them out.

It took us only five minutes to find it. I happened to be the one to hit on it, but even an idiot could have spotted it.

I sat back in my chair and fired up a tabstick. "We've found him."

"Well, what is it—?"

"Tell me what—"

"Do you want us to—"

"*As you were.*" The Sergeant's voice cut through the chatter. "Keep still. General?"

"It says, and I quote, 'The Vators are headquartered behind an abandoned storefront at Thirty-fourth and Third; the sign on the storefront says only *Diane Emmett and Son.*'"

Zev threw back his head and laughed. "That old bastard."

Dov didn't say anything. Words couldn't hurt.

Shimon Bar-El's family name—and our clan name, for that matter—is Bar-El, Aramaic for 'Son of God.' The one and only God is known by a variety of names: Adonai, meaning Our Lord, is one of the most common. Another is the True Judge, Dayan Emet.

Diane Emmett and Son. Shimon had hung up a sign saying where he was.

"Zev?"

My partner nodded. "We need a recon, and bad. What's the neighborhood like?"

"There are enough blacks in it. You won't be too conspicuous. Bring back some good pictures, and don't get into trouble."

"Will do. You?"

"Until we figure out exactly what's going on there, I can't think of anything useful to do except healing, and talking to Paulo Stuarti."

CHAPTER
TEN "Over to You"

The last time I'd seen Paulo Stuarti was on a dusty road outside Anchorville, his field ODs caked with a lot of mud and a little blood—not his; things had gotten a bit raw for a moment. He'd been a lieutenant then, exec in the Casa company Ari was commanding at the time. My brother thought well enough of him to put his own life, as well as Shimon's, Dov's, and mine, on the line, and had later talked Shimon and Giacometti into pushing through a field promotion to captain, leaving Stuarti in charge of the company when Ari left.

His drinking had been under control, or so it seemed. Stuarti made major toward the end of the war, one of the youngest infantry majors that the Casalingpaesesercito ever had. More than ten years later, he was one of the older majors in the Casalingpaesan army.

He sat in an immaculate blue semi-dress uniform in one of the bars off the main lobby of the hotel complex, toying with the ornate aiguillette of a senior aide-de-camp and drinking offworld Scots whiskey, every once in a while examining the bottom of the glass as though there were some great secret hidden there.

He was a big, blond man, which always surprised me; I think of people of Italian stock as being dark and Mediterranean.

He smiled when he saw me. "Ah. Ari's big brother. How are you, General?" He beckoned to the bartender. "Another one of these, and bring the general one of whatever."

"Inspector-General. And I'll take the same," I said.

The bartender brought fresh glasses and set them down on real lace coasters, then moved quickly out of earshot.

We drank in silence for a moment.

"If your brother's not well and you haven't told me already, then you and I are definitely *not* going to get off to a good start," he said, looking off into the distance.

"He's fine. Just back from Thuringia. He's a light colonel now. Probably get his third leaf this year."

"And his stars as soon after that as possible." He nodded. "How have you been?"

I shrugged. Not a good idea; a man with a broken rib shouldn't shrug. "You know us staff types. Nothing terribly exciting. You?"

"Staff types." He rolled an ice cube around in his mouth before spitting it back into the glass. "Staff types," he said again, not liking the taste any better with a cold tongue. "Despite the aiguillette, I am probably the worst staff officer in the history of the Casalingpaesesercito. Only good at one thing, and it looks like I may have a chance to be good at it again."

He smiled and then he drained his glass, beckoning to the bartender for a refill. "The general has promised me a brevet and a battalion when war breaks out. He says 'if,' but he means 'when.' "

"Congratulations." I sipped my whiskey. "Practicing?"

For a moment I thought he was going to hit me, or at least try to. Then he laughed. "Oh, you do that polite scorn very well, Tetsuo Hanavi. Tell me, if war breaks out, am I going to be seeing the magen David over my sights?"

It surprised me for a moment that he used the Hebrew term for the shield of David, but he had served with my brother.

"Possibly," I said. "Unless your ambassador starts talking sense. Nervous about it?"

He laughed. "Nah. Not me. Give me half a year to train a battalion, and your line troops won't want to cross us. Count on it, Inspector-General." His fingers were wrapped around the glass. For a moment, the knuckles whitened, but then the hand unclenched.

"Fair enough. And now that we're done pounding our chests at each other, can we have a civilized drink, if not a civilized talk?"

"Sure," he said. He was silent for a long moment. "So you want me to talk some sense into the ambassador, eh?"

"I don't see any harm in it."

"Don't be silly. He's not going to understand. If you haven't fought with or against Metzadan line troops, it's hard to tell the difference between what you people do and what a private company's going to do. He's been talking to a Neuheimer colonel something-or-other. Bugger's got his own private merc army—a reinforced regiment, I think."

I shrugged. "And who does he register his complaint with when the Neuheimers make a better deal with the Freiheimers, and then turn on your troops?"

He smiled. "You don't understand the system. That's a military responsibility, not a civvy one. Besides, I think the idea of putting a Neuheimer up against a Freiheimer tickles his fancy." He looked into his glass. "Fucking Germans, they're all fucking Germans."

"You've spent too much time around my uncle."

"And your brother. But, like I said, don't try to convince me. Nobody listens to General Giacometti's drunk aide."

The bartender refilled his drink; Stuarti sipped some and wobbled on his stool before righting himself. "Last thing: you can't tell Ambassador Adazzi anything—you have to show him. You got a way to do that?"

I looked long and hard at the bottom of my own glass, but I didn't see any wisdom there.

Maybe you had to filter it through more whiskey. "Another one, bartender. And yes, Major, I just might. Probably within the city, and, if so, it'll be within the next couple of days."

"Really." He set his glass down and eyed me blearily. "And you're enlisting some help in bringing him into viewing range, eh?"

"Maybe. Can I let you know later on?"

He nodded. "Yeah."

"Next question: can I count on you?"

"Who the fuck knows?" He shrugged. "Yes. No. Maybe. Give it a try. See what happens."

I remembered a dusty road outside Anchorville, and a wry grin across Stuarti's face when my brother put all our lives between Stuarti and the Casa Loyalty Detachement troopers who were going to shoot him for being drunk on duty. And I remembered what Ari had said to him, just before the shit hit the fan.

" 'You'll keep that goddamn hip flask in a buttoned pocket until further notice, Lieutenant Stuarti,' " I quoted.

His face was rock-still as he decided how to take that. I didn't make it any easier when I picked up his glass and poured the Scotch onto the bar, then set it down in front of him.

"You're just going to be an observer, Stuarti, but you're going to be a sober one."

"Fuck you," he said, as I turned and left the bar. If he called for the bartender, I didn't hear it.

Back at our suite, Zev was going over a set of maps with the Sergeant and Menachem Yabotinsky when I walked in.

"The Vators got themselves a darned good adviser, who lives in their clubhouse," he said, looking up at me. "There's no way in but through the storefront. Ditto for a way out. Everybody who does business in that neighborhood pays taxes to the Vators, and you meet them at their place. If they come to you, you want to be running."

"Any chance of smuggling in some weapons?"

He shook his head. "No. None. They'll frisk us before they let us in, and even if we're running the gun salesman routine, they're not going to let us hold onto a sample. No easy way."

"You sure Shimon's there?"

"I saw them take him for his evening constitutional, Tetsuo. Two Vators did a recon, then reported back. A while later, a full twenty of them walked him around the block, while everybody on the street buttoned up their windows. Your guess is to how much they were there to stop him from leaving, and how much they were there to keep anybody else from taking him out. They may not know just how valuable the old man is, but they've got an idea."

I nodded. It was about as I'd figured. And about as bad as I'd figured.

Shimon had been able to smuggle some information out, but either hadn't tried to get out the precise details of who he was and where he was, or hadn't been able to. Much more likely he hadn't tried; Metzada wouldn't need it noised about that one of our own, even an exiled one of our own, was working to build up the fortunes of a gang.

So he had assumed that the old woman would send me, and somehow or other he had gotten a message to Dunfey, suggesting that the great youth gang expert, Tetsuo Hanavi, was on his way.

Which helped to explain where we were, but didn't do anything to suggest where we ought to go from here.

"Anybody got any bright ideas?"

The Sergeant licked his lips, then took another pull at his tabstick. "You want some good advice from your old tactics teacher, Inspector-General?"

I nodded.

"Stop squirming around it. Turn it over to me."

There's an old principle we use in Metzada, that the person

most qualified to take tactical command takes it. It's the job of
the commander in charge to figure out who that is.

I didn't have any choice.

It was the Sergeant's job now, not mine.

"It's a bit more complicated," I said. "I've got to get Dunfey
to keep police floaters off our tail while it all happens, and
we're going to want the Casa ambassador across the street or
something, as an observer. We're going to have to do something about making the police prefect out to be the hero of the
thing, too."

"I can work with that." The Sergeant nodded. "Fine by me.
You just line them up across the street." He tapped at the
map. "That hotel there should do. We set things up in there,
and then we walk down and across the street to where they
are, and then we walk in. We can't play this as one of those
split-second coordination specialties. Going to be basic and
simple."

He waited, patiently.

"It's yours, Sergeant," I said. "Over to you."

"Tomorrow morning," he decided. "Tomorrow morning, you
set up your observers and the police cover." The Sergeant
stood. "Rent two rooms in the hotel, and then get them into
the hotel quietly. We'll all move out from there. There's only
one way to get him out. We walk in there, unarmed, into what
I figure is going to be a gathering of at least twenty, thirty,
armed and twitchy little hoodlums, and we get him out."

He looked at me long and hard. "We can't take everyone in.
Dov's pushing it, but we need somebody to watch out for
Shimon when it all hits the fan. I'd like Zev there, but we'll
leave him and Imran for the reserve. Eph'll like that. Inside is
you, me, Dov, Bernstein, Nakamura, and Stern."

Yabotinsky bit his thumbnail and considered the ragged
edge. "And me," the bald little man said, quietly. "And me."

"And Yabotinsky. You keep them talking, and you leave the
rest up to us." His hand shook only fractionally as he reached
for another tabstick. "You just leave the rest to us."

CHAPTER ELEVEN Killing Ground

Thellonee, New Britain
1628 34th Street, New Portsmouth
01/13/44, 0923 local time

Assistant Prefect Nigel Dunfey was unimpressed as he sat back in the overstuffed chair. I could tell that he was unimpressed because his eyes were narrowed and his thin lips were pursed in a frown. I could tell that the chair was overstuffed because somebody had once spent some time with a knife, hacking at it to relieve the condition.

He shook his head. "I find it difficult to agree to give those orders, Inspector-General. Telling the district constabulary commander to keep his men away from here? No matter what happens?"

He looked at the other men in the dingy room of the even dingier hotel. "One would almost think you were planning some sort of military assault, except that I know you are all unarmed, and . . ." He couldn't find a polite way to say the obvious, that the Sergeant and the other oldsters would stand no chance against young hoodlums in peak condition, so he just gestured at the Sergeant and the other oldsters and left it at that.

I gave it another try. "You've got a serious gang problem

here, Prefect. There'll be a whole stack of flimsies with a whole pile of recommendations a couple of weeks after I get back to Metzada"—*and have my number one assistant distill and regurgitate some platitudes into a format that you won't mind paying for*—"but right now, I can tell you what one problem is: the Vators have hired an offworld consultant, too. We're just going to walk on in, and take him out. Period. That should make things a bit easier for you, at least in terms of this gang."

He was about to open his mouth to protest, so I raised a hand. The last thing I wanted was for him to argue himself into a corner that he wouldn't want to back out of.

"It seems to me that if you're going to be paying the kind of money that we're going to charge you, then you really ought to take our advice about the small things, if not the large ones."

He was wavering, so the Sergeant threw in a friendly smile and an open-handed gesture. "What kind of trouble do you think we're going to get into? We're just a handful of men, unarmed." He opened his coat to show just how unarmed he was.

I let the conversation flow around me while, on the street below, a skimmer pulled up to the curb and settled itself down. Three men got out: Zev, Paulo Stuarti, and Adazzi, the Casa ambassador. Dov was waiting for them at the curb; he led them into the building. We had another room rented for them to watch from. More listen than watch, really, and more to wait until it was time for them to come in to watch Zev and Imran pick up the pieces than listen.

"But *how* are you going to get him out? That's what I don't understand. Maybe you don't realize how dangerous those . . . children are. They're not really children, the bloody little savages."

The Sergeant chuckled. "Nothing to worry about. We'll just walk in, let them scare us a bit, then let them talk themselves into letting us go, together with their adviser. No problem. Do scared for him, Yehoshua."

Frail, white-haired Yehoshua Bernstein trembled, his lower lip quivering, for just a moment, until he stopped and smiled.

"Don't worry about it, Prefect," Bernstein said.

"Then why do you want to be certain you won't get help?"

I spread my hands. "It's just that if they do decide to, say, fire off a few rounds in order to get us trembling, we don't want to have to worry about a flying squad of proctors crashing through, and getting them all nervous." I smiled. "I'm a staff officer, myself, and I don't like having any armed man nervous."

"Well . . ." he *tsk*ed a couple of times. "It's against my better judgment. You could get hurt. But it is your choice. . . ." The prefect took out his phone and snapped it open, then issued a few blunt orders. "Yes, that's for the next hour. After that, I'll call you and advise. Dunfey out."

His phone snapped shut just as Imran's hypo hissed against his upper arm; Dunfey started to struggle, but the medician tripped him into the Sergeant's waiting arms, the two of them lowering him efficiently to the floor as the drug took effect.

Imran quickly searched the prefect, coming up with a compact wiregun and two spare clips. "Colt WireKing," he said, tucking it into his belt, quirking his lips for a moment before he stowed the clips in his right rear pocket. "Not a bad little wiregun," he said as he smiled down at the unconscious policeman. "Going to be a hero, you are."

The Sergeant shook his head. "Not if somebody notices that gas-hypo bruise on his upper arm."

"What bruise? I don't see any bruise. All I see is a heroic wound." Imran had already unrolled his medikit and selected a scalpel. "The hero got injured, that's all."

The Sergeant nodded judiciously. "Not enough, though. Give him a wound in the belly, too. Make sure the hole goes all the way through; wouldn't want them to find the wrong bullet inside."

"Aw, Tzvi, that's—"

"—how we're going to do it."

I straightened myself. "I'd better go speak to the ambassador. Take care of things here."

Ambassador Gianpaulo Adazzi was not happy as he paced back and forth in the other room we'd rented, on the floor below. "I don't understand what I'm doing here. Major Stuarti practically *forced* me into the skimmer, and . . ."

"And brought you here to see a demonstration," I said. "The word is you're thinking of hiring some private company, instead of Metzada." I shrugged. "Makes no difference to me, personally, which side of the war we come down on," I lied. "But I thought you might want to watch a little demonstration."

I jerked my thumb at the window. "Across the street and down the block is the headquarters of a youth gang called the Vators. There are about twenty, thirty of them in there right now, many of them armed. One of the reasons they're in ascendancy over the other local gangs is that they've managed to get some guns."

"Oh?" He was starting to get interested, despite himself. "Just one of the reasons?"

"Yeah. It's the secondary one, matter of fact." I made him wait while I pulled out a tabstick and fired it up. "Also in there is an exiled Metzadan citizen, name of Shimon Bar-El. You may have heard the name. Seems that he took on a job as a tactical adviser to the Vators, and they're not eager to let him go."

The ambassador shrugged. "Why not make them an offer for him? I'm sure they could use money."

There wasn't any threat in Dov's voice as he said, "We don't do that. We don't buy our people back with money." If I hadn't known him better, I would have been worried by his flat tone, by the blank way he looked at the ambassador, as though ticking off kill-points on an anatomy chart.

But I did know him better. Shimon wasn't interested in Dov taking offense at mere words.

Adazzi raised an eyebrow. "It can't be that policy dating back to the twentieth century, can it?"

"Thirteenth," I said. "Agree with it, disagree with it, but get your centuries right. In 1286, the German emperor imprisoned Rabbi Meir ben Baruch of Rothenburg—for trying to emigrate to Eretz Yisrael, by the way. Rabbi Meir died in prison seven years later, not allowing his people to ransom him, for fear of setting the wrong kind of precedent. Rabbi Meir's precedent has been broken too often since. It won't be broken here and now."

Adazzi nodded. "So you're going to break out Shimon Bar-El. Where's the rest of your force?"

I smiled. "He's upstairs, probably putting his medician's kit back together. No, Ambassador, it's just us. One good master private, a staff officer, and five old, retired soldiers are going to walk in, and take him out."

He smiled at that. "What's the trick?"

I smiled back at him. "There isn't one."

The outer room had been a shop of some kind, once; against the gray wall, empty, dusty cases stood, displaying their invisible wares to ghosts.

Four of the Vators stood the six of us against a wall. They frisked us thoroughly, professionally, a sharp-eyed fifteen-year-old going through our overcoats inch by inch. Beyond them, a steel door stood shut, grillework about eye-level, ragged weapons ports quite probably concealing pistol barrels.

There was a metallic taste at the back of my mouth; I swallowed to get rid of it, but it didn't go away.

"They're clean, Michael," the boy said, turning his head to the grille.

"Well, then, let them wait for a while," sounded from beyond the grillework. "We're doing some business here."

In the distance, I could hear a familiar voice. "The thing you're going to have to learn, Michael, is that justice isn't done in the dark. That's part of the difference between becoming a government and remaining a gang."

None of us looked at each other, but Yehoshua Bernstein leaned against the wall, and was immediately prodded to uprightness by the pistol-barrel of the weasel-faced teenager at his right.

There was a long pause. "Well, search them again, and then let them in."

The room was larger than I'd expected; they'd cut through the wall between two buildings and made one large assembly hall, a hundred yards across and twenty deep.

Over against the far wall, a haphazard pile of mattresses was stacked alongside neat pyramids of water bottles and food tins. The Vators didn't look like they were planning for a siege, but it looked like they were ready for it, with troops as well as provisions: there were thirty-seven Vators in the room, split about three-to-one male, with a few cases in doubt.

Including the guards keeping an eye on us, I could count eleven guns: ten slugthrowers, only one wiregun. Except for our guards, all the weapons were tucked in belts or holsters, which was good. The gunmen were pretty much randomly scattered about the room, some sitting in stolen chairs, others sprawled on mattresses.

Three of the gunmen were girls, or female at least. They had that hard, I'll-slice-the-skin-off-your-face expression that offworld women get when they spend too much time around violence.

It looked like the Vators were holding a trial. It was easy to figure out who the accused was: he was tied to a chair. He sat halfway across the room, one of four people in a row of chairs next to a battered gunmetal-gray desk. Behind the desk was a vicious-looking boy of maybe eighteen, holding a Webster Multi wiregun pistol by the barrel, using it like a gavel. His face was thin and pocked, but his eyes moved slowly across us, as if he could see all the way through to what we really were.

For a moment, his eyes rested on mine. A hero would have returned his stare, would have manfully looked him in the eye, but I was just a cowardly gun-merchant, hoping to leave this room with both a deal and my skin, so I swallowed and looked away.

"All right, all right, shut up, everyone." He gestured toward us with the butt of the gun. "We'll be done with this in a few minutes. Until then, you just stay lined up and out of trouble—then we can talk some business." He turned to glare at the old man sitting in the middle of the group in front of him. "That good enough for you, Shimon?"

Shimon Bar-El smiled casually. "You're the boss, Michael. But it's fine with me." He looked a bit thinner, a bit paler, a bit older since the last time I'd seen him, but he hadn't changed much.

Of the four sitting next to the desk, Shimon was the only unworried one. At Shimon's left were a fiftyish, red-headed, red-faced man and a red-headed, teen-aged girl who might have been pretty if the right side of her face weren't black and blue, her right eye swollen almost totally closed. There was a long scratch on her neck that ran down from just below her ear and into the gray blanket she huddled in.

The man had a protective arm around her, although what good that would do escaped me.

A hero would have made a mental note to himself to drag them to safety when all hell broke loose, or at least to shout a warning, but I'm just a butcher.

On Shimon's right, the accused sat, bound efficiently to a chair, his ankles drawn back and tied to the rear legs, his hands bound forward. As he shook his head to clear the stringy blond hair out of his eyes, he looked more defiant than scared—but it was a close call.

Michael turned to us. "We're having a bit of a trial here. Although I'm not really sure why we're just trying Kevin, here."

There were nods and grunts of agreement from around the room.

"Excuse me," I said.

The guards started; Michael stilled them with a wave of his hand. "Go ahead."

"If you want us to come back later, we're at your disposal."

He gave a grin that he probably thought was wolfish. "You don't want to be around for this?"

I shook my head. "I don't mind, either way. But if you want us to stay, then you probably should let us know what this is all about."

He thought it over for a moment, then nodded. "Kevin was—is one of my squad leaders. We're discussing a complaint here that his squad dragged Fiona here off the street to pull the train."

He looked at the girl; she hid her face in the blanket and huddled closer to her father.

"And a fun little train-pull it must have been. That's not the problem."

He paused for a moment to stare at a group of six boys and three girls who were off by themselves in the corner of the room, away from the rest. None of them were armed, and at least two of the boys were a little wild-eyed, but the other four boys and all three of the girls had gotten the point that only Kevin was on trial.

"Fiona," he went on, "is the daughter of old man Foster, here, who has a tucker shop just inside of Vator territory. You pay your taxes regular, Foster?"

The red-headed man nodded, once, quickly. "Yes, yes, I do, I do—"

"Shut up."

The red-headed man shut up.

"Now," Michael went on, "Shimon here says that since we Vators are on our way to becoming a government, we're supposed to give something for the taxes we collect." He rose and walked over to Fiona and her father, putting a hand under her chin and looking her face over very carefully. She stared back at him, a rabbit looking at a snake. "I sort of like being a government, if I'm going to have to live the rest of my life in this shithole of a neighborhood."

"You can be what you want to be. Governments have started

the way you are." Shimon Bar-El spread his hands. "But if you are a government, then you have to protect your peasants. It would be one thing if they'd snatched a girl from off-turf. But she's a local, and they knew it."

Michael laughed as he let the girl's head drop. She huddled even closer to her father.

"Fair enough. But then why don't I put all the squad in the dock?"

"Because you can't." Shimon smiled. "Because you can't afford to lose ten of your people in the first place. In the second, it wouldn't be just ten, because Kevin's squad won't hold still for you cutting all of their throats—you'd lose some from your other squads, too. In the third place, it wasn't their fault. It was Kevin's job to keep them off local girls, not theirs. They were under his authority; it was his responsibility."

Michael smiled again. I was beginning to dislike that smile. "So it's his neck. You got anything to say for yourself, Kevin?"

"Mike, Mike. You can't. I'm your *friend*, dammit, I'm your—"

"Shhh . . ." Michael said. Steel flickered in his hands.

"C'mon, Michael, you can't do this to me, dammit you can't do this you can't—"

Michael shut him off with a backhanded slap to the face. He rubbed at his knuckles. "You stupid shit. Told you to keep off of the local girls."

"M-Mister Michael," the shopkeeper stuttered, "can we go now?"

Michael smiled again. "No, no. It was your daughter Kevin raped. You get to cut his throat." He picked up the shopkeeper's right hand and placed the knife in it. "Right, Shimon?"

My uncle shrugged. "It's safer for all. Makes him a participant, instead of just a witness. Not that anybody'll care, one way or the other. It's the advantage of disciplining your own people: outsiders don't care what you do to each other."

"Then it would make sense to have these others help, too."

"Eh?"

"Make them participants, too." Michael said. "Instead of witnesses."

Bar-El smiled. "It would, at that. Although I don't see the need. Once you and they finish doing business, they're likely to be long gone." Shimon jerked his head at Dov. "You. The big one. You mind helping in a bit of butchery?"

Dov shrugged. "Sure."

Michael shook his head. "Nah. Not him. One of the old ones—you," he said, beckoning to Yehoshua Bernstein. "You come over here and help. And then we can all sit down and talk some business."

Like an old man on the verge of fainting, Yehoshua started to sway. One of the guards prodded him with his gun. That was his last mistake.

Everything flew apart at once.

Without warning, without any preliminary, Yehoshua turned, reached out a finger and stuck it in the boy's eye, bursting it like a grape.

The guard screamed. Reflexively, he reached both hands to his face, his grip on his pistol loosened; Yehoshua wrestled it away from him.

He brought it up and started firing.

Neither of the guards near me had a pistol, but one had raised a stick; I ducked underneath and slammed the edge of my hand into his windpipe, crushing it as shots began to echo hollowly throughout the hall.

The hoodlums were tough, and their reflexes were those of youth, but they never had a chance.

They were used to set-piece battles, where everyone knew a fight was about to happen, and to jumping unsuspecting victims. They weren't ready for the old wolves. A wolf attacks the enemy that's the most dangerous to the pack, not to himself.

As red flowers burst from his belly and chest, Yehoshua was already emptying the pistol, not at those who were shooting at him, but at the armed hoodlums nearest to Yabotinsky and Stern.

Moshe Stern was already in a flat dive; rolling, he picked up the gun of an injured boy, half rose, and started picking out targets, stomping once on the boy's face to quiet him.

The Sergeant had spun around to grapple with the hoodlum behind him. He smashed his forehead into the boy's nose, then twisted the gun out of the hoodlum's hands, sliding it across the floor toward Menachem Yabotinsky as three shots shook his body. He crept across the floor toward the barred door, leaving a red trail behind him.

Michael jerked the wiregun from his waistband, but Shimon tripped him and then Dov was on him, moving faster than anybody has a right to. He slapped Michael across the throat, once, and yanked the wiregun from the boy's hand. Michael staggered to the side, clutching at his crushed trachea, gasping, trying to get some sound, some word out, but he was dying as he fell to his knees.

Dov scooped Shimon up and half-carried, half-threw him under the desk, out of the line of fire, and turned to face two of the young hoods, who were already upon him, each with a knife in hand.

He shifted his weight to the balls of his feet and shrugged past their lunges, moving fluidly, gracefully, like a dancer, as he smashed one in the face with his left elbow, then reached for the other one with his right hand. He barely seemed to touch the other, but the boy spun away, spitting blood and teeth, jerking spasmodically until he collapsed a few meters away.

Dov was bringing up the wiregun when a half-dozen gunshots caught him, one smashing his jaw into a red pulp, another knocking his knee out from under him, yet another slamming into his chest, bringing him down.

A hero would have done something about the girl and her father, but I was fighting for my own life when one shot splashed her blood and brains across her father's chest and face, followed by a flurry that cut off his anguished screams.

Yehuda Nakamura was using his second captured gun,

carefully taking aim at each of the young gunners in turn. There had been three of them in the far corner; by the time Menachem Yabotinsky and Stern had reached them, all three were down, one dead, the other only wounded.

Yabotinsky and Stern had retrieved the captured firearms and begun shooting, but it was almost all over. All of the gunmen had been taken down, and Menachem Yabotinsky and Stern simply blew away anyone who made a motion toward any of the half-dozen guns lying on the bloody floor.

"Stay the fuck *away* from the guns or you're *dead*. Hands *up*, assholes. Get your fucking hands *up*," Menachem Yabotinsky shouted, his shouts cutting through their screams and whimpers. It was the voice of a man decades younger—strong, uncompromising.

Three of our dead and easily four times that many of their dead and dying littered the floor; it was almost over.

The Sergeant lay near the door, now unbarred.

It had started, and it was over, in seconds.

Firefights are like that; even the most active of elite troopers spends less than one percent of their active duty time near shots fired in anger.

The room stank. All of the dead and most of the dying had voided themselves, in the mindless reflex that all animals use to leave themselves unappetizing to their predators.

"Get your fucking hands up, and get over against the wall," Menachem Yabotinsky called out again.

There were only ten or so uninjured; Vators shouted incoherent surrenders, moving quickly, faces pale.

As he worked his way across the blood- and shit-slickened floor, Moshe Stern carefully shot through the head a boy whose outstretched hand was too close to a loose pistol; the shot echoed loudly through the hall, but the cries of the surviving Vators almost drowned it out.

Stern stooped to pick up the pistol. A dark stain spread across his belly as he crouched.

The steel door to the outside creaked open and Ephraim

Imran entered the room with a dive-roll-and-recover that would have done credit to a much younger man, and then rose to his feet, tracking Dov's Korriphila across the carnage. He was followed immediately by Zev, who rose to his feet in a half-squat, Dunfey's stolen pistol held out in front of him, Imran's medikit strapped tightly to his back.

It was almost all over.

Shimon was kneeling over Dov. "Medic, here," he said.

"In a sec." Ephraim Imran dropped a hand to the Sergeant's neck. "Shit. Tzvi's dead."

"Move your ass, man," Yabotinsky said. The balding little man wasn't interested in displaying emotions.

Imran was already working his way past Yehuda Nakamura's and Yehoshua Bernstein's bodies before joining the old man over Dov.

I'd finished off my own two adversaries seconds ago, eons ago, and had stooped to recover the leader's wiregun from where Dov had dropped it.

"Shut up, all," Menachem Yabotinsky shouted, his eyes fixed on the Vators crowding against the wall.

"Tzvi?" he asked, more out of long-established practice than any belief that the Sergeant would still be alive.

No answer.

The Sergeant's body was over by the door that he had unbarred. I walked to him and covered his face. It wasn't right that the rest of them should look at him like this.

Zev laid a hand on my shoulder, but I shrugged it off.

"Moshe?"

"Gut shot," Stern said, easing himself down to the floor, the barrel of the gun never drooping. "I can manage."

Some of the Vators were screaming and some were shouting, but it all blended together in a mess of sound.

"Yehuda?"

No answer.

"Yehoshua?" Old Yehoshua lay where he had fallen, unmoving, his eyes distant.

Again, no answer.

"Dov?"

"Stable," Imran said. "I think he'd going to make it, although he's going to need a lot of work. He's got a sucking chest wound, but it's the right side." He and Shimon crouched over the big man. "Bring him in," he called.

"Tetsuo?" Menachem Yabotinsky called out, not taking his eyes from the Vators huddling in the corner.

"Unhurt," I said, realizing that I was lying when I noticed that I was pressing my hand to my aching side. I'd probably worsened the broken rib. But I'd been lucky. The Vators had concentrated on shooting targets, and left me to take out my two guards without being shot at much. I had a dim memory or something whizzing past my ear, but whoever it was hadn't been allowed any more shots.

"Tetsuo, if you're unhurt, I got something for you to do." Imran didn't raise his head as he worked over Dov.

"What do you need?"

"I've got the prefect stashed in the outer room. Drag the hero in here, will you?" He tossed a hypo at me. "Give him this, right on the wound on his arm."

"Will do."

From behind me, I heard a familiar voice. "Stuarti," the major said, announcing himself. "Safe to come in?"

Menachem Yabotinsky was still in charge. "Come," he said. "Tetsuo, watch them."

As I turned, I took another look at the bodies of the father and daughter. It occurred to me that if I'd killed Shimon when I was supposed to, back on Indess, I wouldn't have to be standing here, looking down into the dead face of a man whose last sensation had been the taste and smell of his own daughter's blood and brains—but then it occurred to me that I didn't really have to look, so I looked away.

Zev and Stuarti led Ambassador Adazzi into the killing ground. Zev held Dunfey's pistol out in front of him, not quite pointing it at anyone as he took in the scene, his face as impassive as Stuarti's. The ambassador was white-faced. Apparently he hadn't seen a lot of dead people before.

"Just old, worn-out soldiers," Stuarti said. "And unarmed."

It really looked more impressive than it was. If we'd given them any warning, they'd have handled themselves better, but it had been easy for the Vators to see a bunch of old men as no threat at all. And there had been no warm-up, no anthropoid chest-beating.

A wrinkled old man had just reached up and stuck his finger in an eye, that was all.

Menachem Yabotinsky was at my side; he held open his hands for the wiregun. The surviving Vators crowded even tighter against the wall, milling like sheep. I handed it over.

"Zev, I'll take the hero's gun, too," he said.

"Officially, Ambassador," I said, "we got into trouble and the prefect saved our asses, demonstrating unusual courage and great blahblahblah. We wanted you to see it unofficially. So you can have some understanding of what you're bidding on. What you can either hire or face . . ."

No, you don't get used to the smell of the dead and the cries of the dying. But there are times when you can affect to be unbothered by it, and wave that affectation in front of a civilian, threatening him with your barbarity.

He tried for a bit of composure, and found it. "Impressive," he said, "I can count twelve of them dead, for only three of yours." He knew it was the wrong thing to say as soon as the words were out of his mouth, but they hung in the air.

Menachem Yabotinsky looked at him. "Twelve for only three. I guess that doesn't impress you enough." Menachem Yabotinsky smiled. It wasn't a grin; it was the rictus a wolf uses, to free his teeth to sink into another's flesh. Adazzi would always remember that smile.

Zev echoed what we all were thinking. "You really shouldn't have said that, Ambassador."

"I count thirty-seven to three," Menachem Yabotinsky said. "And no matter, we would have had to use Dunfey's gun a few times, anyway."

"What do you mean—?"

Menachem Yabotinsky brought up both wireguns, and thumbed them both to full automatic.

It wouldn't have made a difference to a military man, but we wouldn't have had to persuade a soldier that Metzada is the best there is. Giacometti and Stuarti already knew just how good we are, but that hadn't convinced Adazzi.

For Adazzi, it had to be something different. Show him a taste, just a little taste of brutality, and then let him think long and hard about what uniforms he wanted men like Yabotinsky to see, as they looked over their sights.

Adazzi raised a hand. "No, *don't*—"

The Vators started screaming.

CHAPTER
TWELVE Company C

It had been a long day and a half since the shooting, most of it spent shrugging. But the local police really had two distinct choices: to see us as rescued victims, and Dunfey as our heroic rescuer; or to see him as a dupe and then try to work out what we were, no matter how bad that made him—and them—look.

Cops protect their own; while the questioning had been lengthy, it had also been pro forma: the still-groggy Dunfey was in line for a promotion, and we were all dutifully grateful to him. I don't know who among the cops really believed the bullshit, but nobody was going to announce that the emperor was butt-naked, so it was all right.

We gathered around the table in the living room of our suite, some of us the worse for wear.

I was the least-injured of the injured, and my retaped ribs were only a distant ache. Dov wasn't with us; he was in the Preserve hospital, in stable condition. The big man was deadly at hand-to-hand, but that doesn't armor anyone against bullets.

Neither does innocence. I guess I should have felt bad about the merchant and his daughter dying, but you get used to that sort of thing; they weren't the first innocents to die in a crossfire, and they wouldn't be the last.

The doctors at the Preserve hospital may have been mainly men, but they did a good job on Moshe Stern, doing a keyhole bowel resection, pumping him full of antibiotics and painkillers, and then releasing him twenty-four hours later—granted, against their advice. He was more propped up than sitting up.

Yabotinsky was just tired. He yawned broadly, scratched at his scalp, then reached for the whiskey bottle, pouring for himself and the other oldsters.

"You sure you should be drinking?" Zev asked Stern.

"No," Stern said, as he reached for his glass.

I turned to Ephraim Imran. "Any chance of Dov being able to travel shortly?"

"Depends what you mean," Imran said. His eyes seemed to have trouble focusing; his voice was ever-so-slightly slurred. "They say I can have him fit for a stretcher tomorrow. He can take a launching, although he won't like it much."

Shimon Bar-El shook his head. "Leave him be. Leave him be. We're not going to need him for the fix I have planned. All we need is a bit of time."

I looked long and hard at my uncle, but he either didn't notice or didn't care.

The Sergeant was dead. He'd loomed larger over my life than almost anybody, including my own father. He'd trained me as a soldier, and had watched my back during my first firefight, way back when.

And I hadn't even been watching him while he died; I'd been too busy trying to kill a couple of seventeen-year-old hoodlums.

There are some things you don't get used to. Having people you love dying on foreign soil is one of them.

Zev seemed unmoved by the whole thing. "Fix?"

Bar-El nodded. "A fix. Actually, you'd be better off giving

me command of the whole Rand campaign, but I knew you wouldn't do it, so I found another fix."

"Who'd you get it from?" Zev asked. "And what is it?"

"You seem to think I'm stupid, but I hope you don't think I'm *that* stupid," Shimon Bar-El said. "For one thing, the walls may have ears. Which is why I'm not going to tell you where I got the other information, other than that it was before I . . . overreached myself with the Vators."

In the back of my mind, I'd been wondering about that, but his explanation made sense. We knew he'd been doing some consulting work; possibly he'd picked up the news about the Freiheimer tanks during that time, before he'd become a prisoner of/adviser to the Vators.

"As to the fix, it's a bit soon to tell you what, but I don't mind telling you where: Alsace."

Alsace.

We all sat silent for a moment. It really didn't matter which campaign Shimon thought he had a fix for; there would have been people we cared about in any. There always are, anywhere Metzada goes.

But *Alsace*. Benyamin was on Alsace, part of the new Eighteenth, under Yonni Davis.

David Alon walked into the silence, a sober grin threatening to become tastelessly broad. "We've wrapped up the contract with Casalingpaesa," he said. "On reasonable terms."

The room probably wasn't bugged, but there was no sense in taking chances. What he meant was *we've got a deal that would be pretty good, even if we didn't know that an armor strike is going to go through Freiheimer armor like hot lead through butter*.

"What kind of force? Did they go for a division, or—?"

"Two. One armor, one line infantry," he said, trying to keep the pleasure out of his voice, failing miserably. He'd been trying to get them to go for *one* division.

"Good," Shimon said. "You're leaving for Metzada tomorrow?"

Alon thought about not answering for a moment, but then he shrugged. "Yes, I am."

"Good, again. Have a message passed to Davis, via the next courier. Just tell him that the IG is on his way. With me in tow."

One of the things about my uncle that always annoyed me was his ability to skip past the preliminaries. It was obvious that he wasn't going to tell us what kind of fix he had planned for the Alsace situation, and that I didn't dare press him too hard—but would insist on accompanying him there.

Alon's face went grave. "We'll be taking the bodies with us," he added quietly. "The Constabulary just delivered them. They're in cold storage in the basement."

"Wait one minute, General." The glaze was suddenly gone from Yabotinsky's eyes. "We do not carry bodies with us. We are buried where we fall. Tzvi, Yehuda and Yehoshua died for Metzada."

It's long been a tradition, ever since David Bar-El created the Metzada Mercenary Corps, that those serving it are buried where they die, not carried back.

Alon shook his head slowly. "It wasn't official, here or home. Officially, here, they were visitors regretfully killed by youth gang members, despite Prefect Dunfey's heroic efforts. Officially, at home, they were retired old soldiers, helping the inspector-general out with a youth-crime survey, not on duty. The Prefecture returned the bodies to us just an hour or so ago, and I don't want to make a fuss about trying to find burial plots here."

The years fell on Menachem Yabotinsky's shoulders, and he was just a bald man sitting uneasily in a chair, too much whiskey muddying his tired brain.

"Eph," he said. "Help me to bed."

He rose, unsteady, and Ephraim Imran was at his side, helping him from the room. Alon opened his mouth, as if he were going to say something, but there wasn't anything to say and he closed it.

"Sit down, David," Shimon Bar-El said, pushing the whiskey bottle to him.

Moshe Stern intercepted it, and poured himself another hefty slug with a trembling hand.

"As Sergeant Aroni was saying, I don't think that's a good idea, not with a healing gut-wound," General Alon said.

Stern sat silently for a moment. "You know, General, I don't give a shit what you think." He knocked back a slug and poured himself another, then slammed the bottle down in front of Shimon Bar-El. "You any good at lying, Bar-El?"

Shimon Bar-El nodded. "Fair. Why?"

"Because you're about to tell me that what you've got in your head is going to save more of our lives than getting you out of there has cost. And I want to see if I can guess if you're lying."

I can't always tell if somebody's lying or telling the truth, but sometimes I can. I knew he wasn't lying when he said:

"It was worth it, Moshe. It was worth it." Bar-El looked him straight in the eye. "Proof of my sincerity, I'm letting the obvious slide by without comment, let it go over some heads here and now."

Stern looked at him long and hard, then nodded and drank some more.

Alon raised an eyebrow. "What did you mean by that, Bar-El?"

Shimon didn't answer.

He never answered when he didn't want to. We'd find out soon enough, probably. I rose and walked to the window, glass in hand.

I looked out into the night. There were no landings scheduled tonight; the field was unlit. The darkness of the Preserve seemed about to reach out and grab at the city. The city probably deserved it.

I turned my back on the night.

Stern set his glass back down on the table, then slumped back in his chair. It was about all he could do; gut wounds take a lot out of you, and he really should still have been in the hospital.

Bar-El turned to Alon. "My regards to the deputy, and tell her to have the way cleared for the three of us on Alsace.

Tetsuo, Zev and I will be relaxing here for a few weeks to be sure the message has gotten through, and then we're on our way—and see if she can arrange a mail drop for the Eighteenth at Circum-Thellonee; we'll carry it."

Zev looked at me, and I nodded. There was no way I was going to get him to tell us what sort of fix he had in mind for the Alsace problem, and if we were to drop blind into that mess, it could be very bad. Too easy for us to be made to disappear—much better to get a bit of a warning going.

We drank and talked aimlessly for a few minutes. There's always something about what you do after a fight that's special, even if what you do isn't particularly special in and of itself. I don't know if that makes sense, but it's always there. The time in the police station didn't count; that was part of the battle, that was among foreigners.

Here was different. Here I was with my own. What was left of them. The Sergeant was dead. I could feel my heart thud slowly in my chest, just the way it did during a NoGain session. Uncle Tzvi had been a pillar in my life, and now the pillar was gone.

They all die on me—my father, my brothers, the Sergeant— the bastards all die on me.

A klaxon started hooting somewhere.

"*Fire alarm, fire alarm,*" sounded from speakers that I hadn't seen, couldn't find even now.

Alon was already on his feet. "What's that—?"

"Don't be an ass, man," Shimon Bar-El said. "I'm surprised it took them so long."

"What?" Alon was halfway to his feet; Shimon waved him back.

"It's been too long for you, David Alon," said my uncle, Shimon.

Below, the darkness was shattered by fire: three coffin-shaped boxes blazing away into the night. Two men, one carrying an improvised spear, stood watch over the fire, probably to make sure that nobody put it out too soon. I hoped nobody would try to get past them. Yesterday had been a special case; I wasn't sure I could clear yet another homicide with the local authorities.

Moshe Stern forced himself to his feet, reeling with the pain. "It's Eph and Menachem," he said. "They're cremating the bodies. I wish I'd been strong enough to help them." He spoke quietly, his voice barely louder than a whisper. "You're not taking their bodies home, General. They will be buried where they fell." His face was unmoving, his voice level as he picked up the whiskey bottle and splashed some of the liquid more at than in the glasses on the table, then dropped the empty bottle to the carpeted floor. "You're senior, Shimon Bar-El."

"So I am." Shimon Bar-El stood slowly. He pursed his lips, opened his mouth, and then closed it. When he spoke, his voice was husky. "Friends, brothers, and cousins, a toast," he said, raising his glass. "To Company C, First Battalion, the old Eighteenth Regiment: the fire burns."

Stern nodded. "Company C."

We all drained our glasses, then shattered them against the wall.

Below, the fire burned a long time.

PART THREE ALSACE

The Lord said to Gideon: "You have too many people with you for Me to let you defeat the Midianites, for your people will think that they have saved themselves. So, tell whoever is afraid to return home, to depart early from Mount Gilead."

Of the people, twenty-two thousand returned; ten thousand remained.

The Lord said to Gideon: "There are still too many. Bring them down to the water, and I will test them there; and I will decide who will go with you."

So he brought the people down to the water, and the Lord said to Gideon: "Everybody that laps the water with his tongue shall be set apart from those that bow down on their knees to drink."

The three hundred men lapped up the water, putting their hand to their mouths; all the rest bowed down on their knees to drink.

The Lord said to Gideon: "With the three hundred I will save you."

—Judges 7:1–7

CHAPTER THIRTEEN Celia von du Mark

The inspector's men hauled the three of us off the shuttle five minutes before it was due to leave, ten minutes before the drop window to Port Marne closed.

Of course, the forms had to be followed. We couldn't be hauled off, not if we'd accept a polite invitation, even though the polite invitation was delivered by five security men.

"Inspector-General Tetsuo Hanavi?" The largest one, a stocky Aryan type, smiled down at me with patently false friendliness; I returned the smile. The collar insignia on his blue coveralls proclaimed him to be a Commerce Department Security man; the five gold service strips on his sleeve said that he had been at it a while.

I nodded. "That's me."

"General Shimon Bar-El?"

"No such person." Shimon shook his head. "Just Mr. Shimon Bar-El. I'm retired." He smiled.

The guard leader didn't see the humor in that, and I wasn't about to spend a lot of time and effort explaining it.

"Sergeant Zev A-runny?" he asked.

173

"Aroni," Zev corrected. "Aroni."

"Yes, sir. Aroni. If you will all follow us, please?"

I eyed the five of them just for practice as we unstrapped ourselves from our acceleration couches. Shimon and I handed our bags to Zev, then we followed the guards back into the Gate complex, one man at my right, one man at Zev's left, Shimon in the middle.

Their training was fair: they stayed close to our arms, the leader in front and the last two guards walking behind, their batons in their hands.

We were neatly hemmed in, assuming that the guards at our sides were willing to take some damage. If we tried to make some sort of break, my guard would grab my arm, Zev's guard would grab his, while the leader and the other two moved in for the kill.

Shimon wouldn't be much of a factor in a fight, and even if he were, it would still be possible for two guards to trip up all three of us while the others took us out with their batons.

Not bad, but not the way I'd handle a guard detail. My feeling is that when it's necessary to guard someone, manners can go out the nearest airlock.

I didn't look at Zev, and he didn't look back at me, but we could have taken them.

"May as well leave the bags in a locker," Shimon said, as we walked through the broad, low-ceilinged concourse.

I paused in front of a battered set of lockers and gestured a question, rewarded by a tolerant nod.

The leader held back a smile. As soon as we were out of the concourse, the lockers would be opened and our gear would get much more than the casual Customs inspection we had already gone through—but we had to maintain the polite fiction that a locker in the Commerce Department's Gate complex was inviolate.

My only regret was that I *hadn't* brought any contraband. Just two spare uniforms, a Fairbairn knife, a combination toiletries and medical kit, a sheaf of letters from home, and a few books, including the copy of Twain's *Life on the Mississippi* that Shimon had made me read on the trip over.

There was something about part of it that seemed strange, but I couldn't put my finger on it.

I wasn't even carrying a pistol—we'd cached some of the Vators' weapons, left some others for the New Portsmouth constables to find—figuring to procure a flintlock dirtside, without the necessity of going through the usual protracted argument about whether or not the weapon was permissible under the restrictive Proscribed Tech list of the planet—in this case, Alsace.

Shimon's insistence to the contrary, that was probably a mistake. A harmless one, this time—but still a mistake. If you don't give the Commerce Department people something to find, they'll just keep looking until they do.

"This way, General Hanavi, General Bar-El, Sergeant Aroni. If you please."

I chuckled. The lower ranks in the Commerce Department are always polite, even when the situation doesn't call for it. Except the peacemakers, of course—and they're only technically part of the Thousand Worlds Commerce Department: their enlisted ranks get their training from the TW Marines; their officers are all graduates of the Contact Service Academy.

We walked into a corridor, slid along a walkway, bounced up a jumpshaft, then eased ourselves down another corridor in low-weight, toward the inspector's office. I understand why the local inspectors tend to put their offices and quarters up toward the hub of their complexes—low-weight is addictive, once you get past the queasiness—but I wish that just *once* I'd be able to confront one under higher gravity. I was raised in Metzada's gravity of twelve hundred centimeters per second squared, and anything less than half of a standard gee makes my stomach tie itself in knots.

We waited for a solid half hour in the inspector's outer office. Zev did some paperwork while Shimon pulled a book out of his shirt pocket, thumbed it on, and pretended to read.

It was Patton's *War as I Knew It*; the unabridged edition, with both the diary entries and the Warczinsky commentaries, which meant that he wasn't really reading: he'd long since memorized that one. I just stared at the walls and tried to gather my thoughts.

I wasn't going to try to hurry them, or complain about the delay; I'd felt the vibration through the deck as the shuttle was booted away, and I knew that we'd have to wait for the next skipshuttle's departure. I once spent an idle hour figuring out how many man-centuries busy people have been kept waiting in bureaucrats' offices. The bottom line is damned depressing.

I didn't have any particular reason to want to be depressed. I was too busy trying to figure out what Shimon was up to, and what I'd have to do about it.

And about him.

There was some fix, clearly. Some cards were hidden up his sleeve, certainly. He had stumbled on some trick that could be applied to the Alsace situation, something that would turn what was going to be an increasingly bad campaign of the French forces against the Dutch Confederation into a victory for the French and Metzada. The question was what it was, and what I'd have to do after he played his hand.

Make it look like an accident, Pinhas Levine had said. *Make it look like an accident.*

Finally, the inspector's secretary beeped, and the door to his inner office slid open. "You may come in now."

At that, I sighed. *Here we go again.*

"Patience, Tetsuki, patience," said Shimon.

Thousand Worlds Commerce Department Inspector Arthur McCawber was a chubby little man, brown hair receding toward the top of his skull; a rather bad case of low-gee acne speckled his face. His handshake was tentative, as though he were afraid that the big, bad Metzadan would crush his fingers to a pulp if he exerted any pressure.

I don't like the short, nervous types with weak handshakes; they tend to sublimate their fear. It almost always comes out in other ways. I also didn't like the way that he only shook hands with Shimon and me, as though the stripes on the sleeve of Zev's khakis made him a non-person.

"I'm pleased to meet you, Inspector," I said, releasing his hand. "But it's not General—I'm Metzada's *Inspector*-General. I'm here to witness the Eighteenth Regiment's fulfillment of its contract with the Montenier colony."

He waved us to seats, two guards taking up positions on either side and one behind. "Or lack thereof," McCawber said. "When last I'd heard, the Dutch still had them bogged down on the banks of the . . . Nouveau Loire."

Shimon raised an eyebrow. "Loire? I thought that the river was generally known as the Neu Hunse. Named after the river in Der Nederlands, Earthside, no?"

"For the time being, that is the name that's being used. But, as soon as the Metzadan Mercenary Corps regains control of the French-chartered region for the French, I expect that the original, French name will become more . . . appropriate." He smiled at his little joke, then sighed. "Quite a mess."

"I've seen worse," Shimon said.

Alsace was a mess, of course. The chartering colony had been French—hence the planet's French name. But the original Montenier colony died off in one of the harsh winters that sweep across Alsace's only habitable continent. The Dutch settlers had managed to hang on, but neither they nor their countrymen back home had the political leverage to get the Montenier charter lifted.

If you're into morality as opposed to legality, you'd probably agree that the Dutch had the better claim: they had managed to survive, and even flourish a trifle—and it was a Dutch settler who had taken the time to examine the properties of hempwood, and turned Alsace from a dumping ground into a financial bonanza for the Thousand Worlds.

And, of course, indirectly stimulated the second wave of French immigration. Old Van Huysen was probably regretting, from the safety of his grave, that he'd discovered that the hempwood tree's fibers were long, tangled monofilament chains with an incredible tensile strength and heat resistance, usable as linings for rocket nozzles or as the basic building material for skystalks on small, low-gee worlds.

His discovery had brought the French back. And, indirectly, brought some employment to Metzada, when the Dutch Confederation started to express its resentment at French taxation of goods flowing south on the Neu Hunse to the launcher.

McCawber went on: "I'm sure you're wondering why I had you taken off of the shuttle."

He was ready for me to snap back at him, so I didn't answer for a moment. Besides, I wasn't at all curious: McCawber's Dutch sympathies were obvious.

Not that I had any complaint about that. My sympathies were similar. And, similarly, beside the point. Since when does your duty have anything at all to do with your personal sympathies?

I looked at my uncle. Since when does your duty have anything at all to do with your personal sympathies?

Shimon Bar-El smiled back at me, as though to say, *Never has, never does, never will.*

I'd let McCawber stew long enough. I dropped a few words into the silence: "You want to negotiate a settlement."

The Commerce Department people *always* want to negotiate a settlement. There's a belief on Metzada that the Commerce Department was actually founded by Neville Chamberlain, but that's a canard. Chamberlain had been dead for a century before even the predecessor to the Commerce Department was founded.

"Obviously." He smiled slightly. "The Commerce Department's only interest is in improving the hempwood trade."

And, as usual, trying to put some shorts in Metzada's circuits, I thought.

Zev didn't see any reason to leave it as a thought. "The hempwood trade. Not Metzada's trade. I get awfully tired of that."

McCawber wasn't used to us. He looked from Shimon to me as though asking which one of us was going to slap this sergeant down for his presumption. Under other circumstances, I might have done that, just to try to build a basis for communication between McCawber and me—which was probably why Zev had spoken out in the first place—

But I couldn't do it in front of Shimon. We tend to behave differently around him. My shoulders pulled themselves back. "Good point, Zev."

Zev sneered for just a moment. "Thank you, General," he said, insincerely.

McCawber's lips were almost white. "Are you suggesting that there's something *wrong* with the Dutch and the French settling their difficulties by negotiation?"

I shrugged. "As I'm sure General Davis told you, that's not what Metzada does. If Phillipe Montenier wanted negotiation, he could have taken it up with you."

He shrugged. "Montenier says that he isn't interested in settlement, just in collecting his taxes on Dutch shipping. I'd hoped that—"

"I'd betray an employer?" I shook my head. "I doubt it."

"I was once accused of betraying an employer, inspector," Shimon Bar-El said quietly. "There wasn't enough evidence to prove it, mind you, but there was enough to have me stripped of my rank and citizenship, and exiled from Metzada." His hand gripped my shoulder with surprising strength. "Don't expect my nephew to put himself in the way of that."

"Metzada has a contract with Montenier," I said. "For the next five-minus-a-fraction standard years, the Eighteenth will do its damndest to keep the lower river under French control." I shrugged. "As far as we're concerned, he can take one hundred percent of the cargo of Dutch shipping, not the seventy-five he's demanding."

I didn't discuss Montenier's response when a Dutch paddlewheel would try to evade the tax; McCawber knew it as well as I did.

But he pressed. "Perhaps you'll consider forfeiting your performance bond, and pulling the regiment off Alsace? I'm authorized to rebate most of the bond. My only interest is in seeing the planet develop, helping them sell enough fiber to bring their technology up to—"

"So what?" Shimon snorted. "Metzada doesn't give a shit what your interests are."

"Shimon." I held up a hand. "Inspector, what if word gets out that Metzada can be bought off? Even by the Thousand Worlds Commerce Department?"

"Really, I am just trying to see if there's a peaceful way to do this, to—"

"You're ignoring the fact that Metzada wants to sell its services elsewhere, is what you're doing," Shimon Bar-El said.

"The matter is closed." I can be diplomatic, when the situation calls for it. It rarely does. "Now, when can we shuttle down? I'm looking forward to getting to work."

He smiled thinly. "Almost immediately. We have a shuttle leaving for—"

His secretary beeped. "Deputy Inspector Celia von du Mark is—"

It shut off as she barged in, her shortish black hair whipping around her face as she squared off with McCawber. "I thought we agreed that my people would go over these Metzadans' gear," she snapped. "They're tricky, Arthur. You can take my word for it."

"Hello, Celia. How are you?" I kept my voice casual.

She hadn't stopped to take a good look at us before; she did now.

"Shimon Bar-El. Aren't you supposed to be dead?"

"It's good to see you, too," Shimon said. "I'm surprised you recognize me in mufti. Flattered, too. You'll remember my nephew, Tetsuo Hanavi. I don't think you've met Sergeant Zev Aroni."

Celia glanced at my collar. "General?"

"Inspector-general, actually. I was just a line colonel when we met, wasn't I? And I seem to recall you were a full inspector; don't quite remember for sure. . . ."

"*I* remember," she hissed. "I was demoted to deputy after

that Indess affair. You and your uncle came close to ruining my career."

I allowed myself a smile.

"You are much too kind," Shimon said. "How do you like your new post?"

Ignoring us, she turned back to McCawber. "I thought we'd agreed that I'd take care of screening the Metzadans' gear. Your monkeys are swarming all over it."

I raised an eyebrow. "Find anything interesting? Someday, I swear I'm going to leave a bomb in a locker—no timing device or anything like that; just a gimmick to set off a kilo of HE if someone opens my bag. Negative feedback can correct many a problem. In fact—"

"Tetsuo. Shush." For a moment, Shimon's eyes twinkled. "Besides, essence of skunk would work better."

"In any case . . ." I stood. "I'll leave you two to your argument. Inspector McCawber, please let me know when we're cleared for the surface." I didn't bother to tell them where I'd be; no doubt McCawber's people would be keeping an eye on me.

He glared at me. "You're cleared *now*. Your shuttle leaves in . . . fifty-three minutes."

"Fine." I glanced down at my thumbnail. "Then we should be in Marne in—"

"Not Port Marne. Port Leewenhoek. All of the shuttles down to French territory are full for the next . . . seventeen hundred hours," he said, clearly picking the figure out of the air. "Perhaps you would prefer to wait? Or would you rather shuttle down to Port Leewenhoek? I'm sure that the Dutch have some things that they would like to . . . discuss with you."

I looked slowly from the guard on my right to the one on my left, then back to McCawber. Clearly, we were not going to be getting on a shuttle into French territory. Not now. And not in seventeen hundred hours, either.

Zev's voice was almost too low. "Maybe there's something you and I should discuss right now, Inspector."

"Shut up, Sergeant," Shimon Bar-El snapped. "We'll take

the Leewenhoek shuttle," he added, said, quietly. "Leewenhoek is just fine."

McCawber didn't know what to make of that. We were supposed to refuse.

"Sounds good to me," I said, nodding.

Celia didn't like it, either. "I'll be going along, Hanavi," she said.

"Be a bit dangerous around me, won't it? An inspector-general is, technically, a non-combatant; officially, the Dutch couldn't touch me or my staff."

I wasn't worried about that; it was the possibility of unofficial touching that bothered me. My experience is that a body cools to room temperature just as quickly when the killing is informal as it does when all the forms have been met.

She shook her head. "I'll have a squad of peacemakers. This way," she said as she turned to McCawber, "I can keep an eye on him. I don't understand people who kill for money."

Shimon looked straight at her. "No, you don't understand," he said.

She snorted. "So be it. I'll be watching you, you can be sure of that."

I forced a smile. "Going to protect me, eh?"

"Don't count on it."

"I'm not," Shimon said.

Neither was I.

CHAPTER FOURTEEN Alsace Landfall

Alsace, Northern Continent
Port Leewenhoek
03/07/44, 1357 local time

From the window of the banking skipshuttle, the four-klick-long runway looked awfully short, awfully narrow. Some trick of color and perspective made it look separate from the green that surrounded the landing field, as though it were a narrow stick that God was going to use to swat us out of the sky.

The ground came up fast, but just when I was sure we were going to smash into the runway, the pilot leveled off, pulled the nose up, and put the shuttle into a nice landing flare.

"Touchdown," the speaker blared. *"Braking."*

The shuttle screamed to a stop on the tarmac, shuddering as if it thought it was going to break up, vibrating so hard that I thought that I was going to lose my lunch or my teeth.

But it didn't and I didn't, and in a few moments we'd rolled to a stop. Blue-suited stevedores wheeled a staircase up to the side of the skipshuttle, and the three of us descended to the black tarmac, Celia and her peacemakers behind us.

Off in the distance, past the end of the runway, I could see the blue water of the Neu Hunse . . . or Nouveau Loire.

A passenger skimmer hissed up behind us, settling onto the rubber rim of its plenum chamber as the driver throttled it back. Zev took a step toward it, but Celia shook her head and her peacemakers glared at us.

"Commerce Department personnel only," she said. "You'll have to make your own way to the docks."

I smiled. "A bit of the treatment, eh?"

She smiled back. She didn't mean it anymore than I did. "I don't know what you mean," she said. "We'll see you at the riverboat, if and when."

"Saddle up," Shimon said, hefting his bag to his shoulder and walking toward the end of the runway, away from the skimmer and the reception buildings behind him.

I caught up with him easily. "You've got the local maps memorized?"

He shrugged, and then smiled. "Of course. Besides, if you had your eyes open, you'd notice that the draglines they use to load shuttles onto the riverboats are over at the end of the runway, so the riverboat is going to have to dock there sometime. My guess is that we'll see some sort of path from the loading dock here to where we can pick up the boat as passengers." He glanced down at his thumbnail. "Let's hurry."

I was about to suggest that it could be days until the next riverboat showed up, but a far-off steam whistle blew from the direction of the river.

Zev laughed. "You prescient?"

"Nah." Shimon smiled. "The riverboat schedule was on a flimsy on McCawber's desk and I'm quite good at reading upside down. It's about two klicks to the docks. Let's step it up."

I can understand why the Commerce Department initially set up their launcher down south, at the mouth of the Neu Hunse: it's always easier, at least technically, to ship downriver than up.

As it turned out, they would have been better off with the port about a thousand klicks north from where the river dumps into the sea; there was nothing in the French territory, to the south, that was worth enough to absorb the cost of shipping it offworld. All the hempwood grows up north; not only will the plant only grow within a hundred meters of the river, but it seems that it needs an occasional cold winter in order to keep its sometimes-commensal, sometimes-parasitic bacterial partner under control.

But once the Commerce Department had built the launcher, they and the locals were stuck with the placement.

That's one of the more reasonable regulations of the Thousand Worlds Commerce Department: while they'll build landing strips for skipshuttles wherever the trade justifies it, the Thousand Worlds supplies one and *only* one laser launcher per colony world. Launching complexes are expensive to build and maintain. Alsace wouldn't have another until they developed the capital for a hefty down payment, and either the technology to support it, or still more capital to finance the import of technicians and equipment.

So while the Dutch controlled the north and the hempwood, the French controlled the south, and their chartered area around the launching port.

Make that "mostly controlled." The Dutch Confederates had made significant inroads into French territory along the river, in an attempt to give their ships free passage through Port Marne to the Commerce Department launcher.

Which was why, of course, that the French had hired Metzada, and why the war in the south had brought the hempwood trade to a virtual standstill, and why a Thousand World Commerce Department inspector had me landed deep in Dutch territory.

And, why, along with Celia and her peacemakers, there was a reception committee of sorts waiting for us at the Leewenhoek docks.

I took a moment to size up the crowd. About four dozen blocky men, mainly middle-aged, but with a leavening of younger ones, all dressed in dull gray shirts and trousers. The hempwood tree's inner bark makes excellent thread, but the locals hadn't developed a dye that would last through more than a couple of washings.

They all carried belt-knives, of course; on a frontier world, you'll more often find a local without pants than without a knife. A dozen of them had rifles as well: flintlocks and wheel locks. Alsace had yet to develop the manufacturing base to produce cartridges, and manufacturing smokeless powder is tricky. But saltpeter, sulfur, and charcoal were easy to obtain locally. For the first, all that's needed is a well-used outhouse: natural deposits and wood provided the other two.

Celia looked at me, her mouth pursed in self-satisfaction. "I guess this is goodbye." She moved off to the side, beckoning at her five black-suited peacemakers to follow.

"Stand aside, General," Zev said. "When it hits, you go over into the water and swim for it."

"Easy, boy," Shimon Bar-El said. "Don't borrow trouble."

"It looks like trouble's going to lend itself without me asking," he said.

I eyed the warehouses around the dock and the paddlewheel steamer, the *Bolivar*.

No good. We'd have to go through the mob to get to the cover of the buildings, and the only way to the boat would be by crossing fifty meters of open dock. Don't be fooled: those primitive rifles can be very accurate. That aside, Shimon was in no shape to run, and if this whole trip made any sense he had the key to the Alsace campaign locked up in his head.

Still, if we could get to the boat, we'd be safe. Even with a war on, it was still in both sides' interests for a neutral ship to be able to carry limited amounts of heavily-taxed Dutch hempwood to Port Marne. Both the French and the Dutch needed the offworld credits to import medical tech and supplies, among other things—so the *Bolivar* and her two sister sidewheelers had achieved a sacrosanct status, backed up, when necessary, by the two turret guns just aft of the bridge.

And even if someone decided to forget the forms, the skipshuttle we'd ridden down on had already been mounted on the rear deck of the *Bolivar* for transport south; the hatch was only about two meters off the deck and standing slightly ajar—and a skipshuttle's skin is tough.

But the boat was just too far away.

I turned to face the crowd.

"We want a word with you," a grizzled, black-bearded man said. While another faced both Zev and Shimon, the bearded man planted himself in front of me and tapped me on the chest with a gnarled stick almost as thick as my arm. "You're with the killers?" He glared at my khakis.

No, I'm not, I was tempted to respond. *I just like to dress up in uniforms.*

I sighed. He wasn't necessarily as stupid as he sounded. It usually takes civilians a while to work up to killing an unarmed man.

"My name is Tetsuo Hanavi. Hanavi family, Bar-El clan. Inspector-general, Metzadan Mercenary Corps. This is Sergeant Zev Aroni, an Aroni of the Aronis. The other is my uncle, Shimon Bar-El. You are?"

"Amos Sweelinck. What are you doing here?"

Another silly question. But it didn't quite seem politic to point that out. "And these are . . . ?" I gestured at the two men at his side.

"Friends. Of mine, and of the Roupers." He tapped me on the sternum, again. Not gently. "I asked you a question."

"We are preparing to get on the boat. Obviously."

Shimon touched my arm, but I'd already seen that behind the crowd, three men in gray shirts and pantaloons had stepped out of the clutter of boxes in front of the nearest warehouse.

Sweelinck tapped me again, his forehead creased in puzzlement. When he hit me, I was supposed to react, not just stand there: attack him, or cringe. Either would set the mob off. It's standard primate psychology.

I don't have any grievance with that; I'm a primate, too. It's just that a professional can't let his reactions be standard.

He sneered. "We know that you want to join up with your French friends—"

"Employers," Shimon said, flatly.

"Eh?"

"Not friends. The French have bought Metzada's services—*not* Metzada's friendship. They—" He swallowed. "*We* don't take our passions to the marketplace."

"Now," I said, "can we just leave it at that? We'll just be getting aboard—"

"No. We can*not* just leave it at that."

The three men behind the crowd took up positions atop a stack of boxes; their compound bows strung, each nocked an arrow. It was about damn time.

I held up three fingers. "Last chance." I tried to swallow, but my mouth was too dry.

Sweelinck took a step forward.

I stepped back, and pointed to Sweelinck and the two men with him.

Zev pushed Shimon over the side of the dock and drew his knife. But he was too slow. A knobby stick caught him across the chest, staggering him; as he tried to bring his knife up, a flash of thunder smashed his face to pulp.

When a powerful compound bow looses an arrow, you don't see the shaft in flight unless you're looking for it; it seemed as though arrows sprouted from the backs of the three men's heads. Sweelinck and the other two crumpled.

I took a step back to dodge a hasty swing, then snatched my knife from my belt while I kicked Sweelinck's body into the crowd. One of the locals was charging me; I stepped aside and slashed him across the throat as he lunged by, then booted him over the side while I grabbed another, this one a boy of about sixteen, by the hair.

I spun him around to serve as a shield. He didn't seem eager to hold still, so I smashed the hilt of my knife against his temple to quiet him down.

He sagged against my chest, supported only by my grip in his hair. I rested the blade against his throat as I faced the crowd. "Three dead, so far. You want more?" I raised my voice. "*Run or you're all dead men.*"

It worked: the mob broke and ran, weapons unfired. No shame there; if they had been ready for a fight, they would have fought. But they were after a simple lynching, not a battle.

One by one the three bowmen climbed down, and then, arrows nocked, they walked over, keeping a careful eye on the three bodies. Too many soldiers have been killed by supposedly dead men.

I let the local boy's limp body fall to one side, then dropped to my knees next to Zev. It wasn't good. The bullet had plowed through his cheek and the roof of his mouth and lodged itself somewhere in his brain—but he was still breathing.

One of the newcomers knelt beside me, laying his bow down as he shrugged out of his pack.

"Corporal Nahum Eitan," he said. "I'm the medician." He unrolled his gear and brought out a scanner. "No good," he said after only a few seconds. He shrugged. "If it was Metzada . . ."

But it wasn't. I squeezed Zev's hand, and I could have sworn he squeezed back, but Eitan shook his head. "My responsibility, sir. I'll call it. What's left of him is hurting, and he's got no chance." He lifted the only red hypo in his medician's roll.

Water dripped on the hot wood next to me as Shimon Bar-El stood there. "Tetsuo—"

"Shut the fuck *up*." They train us in Section. I should have been able to say that Zev was my partner and my friend, but I wasn't allowed to say the first, and the second wasn't true, so all I could say was, "He's my sergeant." I held out my hand, took the hypo from Eitan and set it against Zev's neck. I triggered it in a single hiss, and then Zev jerked once and fell still.

Gently, carefully, I handed the hypo back to Eitan, and stood. The knees of my uniform were wet with Zev's blood. I'd have to change when we got aboard, and I might as well throw these trousers away. It's hard to get the blood out.

The oldest of the three newcomers, a lanky man with a

badly scarred forehead, stood in front of me. He didn't salute; we're not much on saluting in Metzada. "Skirmisher-Sergeant Sid Levin, sir."

"You took your time," I said, pleased to find that I could still punch for a calm voice and get it.

"The general told us to stay out of it unless and until I was sure you couldn't handle the situation by yourself."

Probably the right move. Probably. We might have been able to talk them out of it, and that would have been better, safer for all.

It wouldn't have mattered, I told myself, looking down at Zev's body. Section men don't die in bed.

"You want us to bring him along?"

I shook my head. Let the Dutch take care of cleaning up the mess. "No, let's get out of here, and on board. Plan on sleeping in shifts. I don't exactly trust those peacemakers."

Levin smiled at the five black-suited men, giving their wireguns a quick glance. His smile could have been mistaken for a friendly grin, if you didn't notice the way his eyes narrowed.

They noticed.

I took a flintlock pistol and powderbag from one of the corpses.

"Do you think, sir," Levin asked casually, "that you could find some use for a handful of wireguns?"

"*No*. And particularly not in front of witnesses."

The youngest of the skirmishers, a blue-eyed boy with kinked blond hair, eyed the bodies of the three dead men. "Standard booty rights?" he asked. He couldn't have been more than seventeen.

I shook my head. "No. Let's get—"

"But we earned—"

"*Save it*," Levin snapped. He shrugged an apology at me. "Sorry, sir. My fault."

I was beginning to like Skirmisher-Sergeant Sid Levin. He took responsibility for his man. He'd probably chew the boy's head off later, out of my sight—but any discipline should properly come from him, not me.

A blast from the boat's steam whistle spun me around, the pistol coming up as if by its own volition.

At the motion, Shimon shook his head. "Asshole. Did you check to see whether or not it's loaded?"

I shrugged. There isn't a way to do that with a flintlock. Oh, you can open the pan to see if it's primed, and you can push the tamping stick down the bore to see if there's something in there, but you can't tell if it's been loaded unless you loaded it yourself.

Which I already knew. I guess I was a bit more shaken than I'd thought. I cocked the piece, then pointed the gun at the nearest of the Dutch corpses before pulling the trigger.

The gun went off with a cloud of acrid smoke, and a loud bang; the body barely shook from the bullet.

"It was loaded," I said, stooping to retrieve a powderhorn and shoulderbag from one of the dead men. "It looks like the captain's a bit nervous," I said. "Let's get aboard."

CHAPTER
FIFTEEN "This Thing that Ruth Did . . ."

Alsace, Northern Continent,
Dutch Confederation Territory
Somewhere on the Neu Hunse
03/07/44, 2207 local time

The nights on Alsace are bright. Its moon is even larger than Earth's, and a trifle closer to Alsace than Luna is to Earth. You'd think that the tides would be the cause of the dramatic rising and falling along the banks of the river—but you'd be wrong. It's nothing so exotic; it's all caused by the spring thawing up in the mountains. While we were well into spring, in some spots along the banks the high-water marks stood two, three meters above low-water.

I stood at the *Bolivar's* stern rail, watching the stars dance on the water behind us, spray from the twin paddlewheels giving me an occasional jolt when the light breeze would catch it and blow it my way.

As we passed by another of the riverfront houses belonging to the wealthier Dutch hempwood planters, the boat slowly turned to follow one of the river's immense curves. It reminded me of a passage from Twain, so I pulled out the copy of *Life on the Mississippi*, and thumbed the pageglow on.

> *The water cuts the alluvial banks of the "lower" river*
> *into deep horseshoe curves; so deep, indeed, that in*
> *some places if you were to get ashore at one extremity of*
> *the horseshoe and walk across the neck, half or three-*
> *quarters of a mile, you could sit down and rest a couple*
> *of hours while your steamer was coming around the*
> *long elbow, at a speed of ten miles an hour, to take you*
> *aboard again.*

I hadn't truly understood that from looking at the topo maps; it had only been an intellectual game.

Here on Alsace, it came alive. As the river turned endlessly, it often would have been possible to leave the *Bolivar* at one of its stops and catch up with it by walking straight across one of the Dutch plantations while the boat followed the twists in the river.

In fact, despite the fact that the paddlewheel was almost twice as fast as the sort Twain described—the boilers were of offworld manufacture, and could easily hold twenty times the pressure—I could have walked the eight hundred klicks from Leewenhoek to Marne in little more than three times the thirteen local days it would take us to steam the distance.

Lay a ruler on the map and it will read out as eight hundred klicks; measure in all the twists and turns, and you'll find that the trip is more than eight times that distance.

Figuring orbits is a lot easier than dealing with a twisting river. . . .

Shimon was standing beside me; I hadn't heard him walk up. That was bad. You should always pay attention. I learned that a long time ago.

A tabstick dangling from the corner of his mouth, he leaned back against the rail. "Sorry about Zev," he said simply.

"Thanks."

He turned and faced the water, and we just stood there for a few minutes, side by side, watching the water and smoking our tabsticks until he said, "Figured it out yet?"

"What?"

"The fix." He blew a puff of smoke out into the darkness, and then tapped a fingernail against the book.

"Maybe." I shrugged. I had glimmerings, but that was all. "Want to tell me right now?"

"Nah. Too tempting." We both considered the churning water below. "Two things you've got to remember, Tetsuki. First is that the Dutch aren't a nation, not here. They're a confederation—during peacetime, the families were feuding with each other more of the time than not." He fell silent.

"And the other?"

He chuckled. "The other is a joke that we both wouldn't find funny." He looked at me a long time. "Sometimes I think you don't even understand yourself, nephew mine."

He was either talking nonsense, or talking over my head. "Maybe so," I said. It seemed like the thing to say. Maybe it was. The sky didn't split open and vomit fire on me. That's always a good sign. "You want to tell me the joke?"

"Eh?"

"The joke, the one I won't find funny."

He considered the end of his tabstick, then threw it overboard. "There was a sport, back in the twentieth century—in the US, pre-NAF—called baseball. Never mind the details—I don't quite understand them myself—but you have to know that the points scored were called 'runs,' and that for a man to score even forty of these points during a whole year was quite good, and nobody had ever scored sixty runs in one year until a man named George Herman Ruth did. You got all that?"

"Baseball. Sixty runs. George Herman Ruth. Got it."

"Good boy. Now the joke: Yankele comes running up to his grandfather. 'Zayde, Zayde,' he says. 'George Herman Ruth just scored sixty runs.'

"The grandfather sits for a long time and thinks, apparently puzzling over something important. Finally, he raises an eyebrow and looks over at Yankele. 'Yankele,' he says, 'this thing that Ruth did—is it good for the Jews?' " He lit another tabstick. "Funny, eh?"

I shrugged. "Not at all."

He smiled for a moment. "Exactly, Tetsuki, exactly. To you and to me, it isn't funny at all." He clapped a hand to my shoulder. "I'll leave you to your reading."

I must have read the next section a hundred times. It was all there. Shimon hadn't distracted me with his joke that wasn't funny. I had it. Even I could turn it all over to Yonni Davis now. There wasn't any more reason to keep Shimon Bar-El alive.

On the other hand . . . maybe I was missing something. I've always been a staff officer, specializing in slipping off and making people unexpectedly dead, not organizing a disperse-and-reform. Maybe I was missing something. And besides, Shimon would be able to implement it better than I could, better than anyone else could.

A while longer. I could let him live a while longer.

There was a whisk of leather soles on the deck behind me. This time I wasn't surprised. I shut the book, trying not to seem too hurried.

"Good evening, Inspector-General." Celia von du Mark stood nearby. Only one of her peacemakers was with her, a careful five paces behind.

The pages were still glowing; I thumbed them off. No need to draw attention to the book. It wouldn't have hurt if she'd read most of it, but the passages I'd been reading . . . well, there were things in there that she didn't need to know.

"Call me Tetsuo." I shot a glance at the upper deck, behind the wheelhouse. Soloveczik, the young skirmisher who had wanted to exercise standard booty rights, was up there, on guard. Well, he might not have been much on discipline, but he was a good shot.

"I'd rather not," she said. "I really don't like getting friendly with murderers," she added, in a voice so flat and even as to suggest that she was commenting on the weather.

"The docks today?" I pulled a tabstick from my pocket and struck it to life. In the darkness, the end glowed with a comforting redness. "That bothering you?"

"Yes." She held out her fingers in a V. I passed her the tabstick and lit myself another. A slow draw, then, "Filthy habit."

"Smoking? Or killing?" I shrugged. "We've got both on our consciences, you and me. If you have a conscience, that is."

"Me?" She was offended; Celia von du Mark was not used to getting lectures on morality from such as I.

"You. You could have had your peacemakers disperse the mob. It might have taken a whole ten seconds. Not that you give a damn about my sergeant, but it would have kept some locals alive."

She snorted. "You know a lot about mobs, eh?"

"Standard part of officer training on Metzada. Now," I said, warming to the subject, "Africans are tricky, but . . . take your basic Eastern mob—Pharsi, Indians, Hmong, Chinese, like that. Present them with a superior force and they martyr themselves all over you. Messy. But when you've got Westerners, almost any organized group can make them run. Usually." I spent a moment examining the glowing head of the tabstick, then flicked it overboard. "Doesn't always work. But it usually does. It would have, today."

"You're saying that I could have saved their lives."

"Exactly. They would have known that they couldn't stand up to wireguns. You," I raised my voice and called out to her guard, "how many rounds do you have in a clip? Fifty? Seventy?"

"Plenty."

I shrugged. "It really doesn't matter. The Dutch would have known that they couldn't stand up to your peacemakers' fire. In order to get the same result out of Levin's three bows, we had to kill."

She was silent for a long moment. Then, "You're just trying to rationalize your way out of it."

"Or you are. Or both. Fact: five men died today. I don't know that the lives of one Metzadan sergeant or a few reasonably nice Dutch settlers are properly any of your concern—"

"Don't you *dare* say that to me. You hated them enough to—"

I silenced her with a snort. "No, I didn't hate them. Matter of fact, Sweelinck impressed me as a good man, trying to make the best of a bad situation. Hell, Celia, if he'd really wanted me dead, I'd be cold by now. Decent man—had to work himself up to it."

"You say you liked him but you had him killed?"

I shrugged. She didn't understand. "One has nothing to do with the other. As I was saying, I don't know if those lives were properly any of your concern, but if they were, then you let your judgment be swayed by an old grudge, by a desire to see me dead, without having the blood—"

"They weren't going to *kill* you! After we left you at the landing strip, I found Sweelinck. They were just going to rough you up a little, scare you off. That's all. And you—"

I snorted. "Don't talk nonsense. Even if that's true, even if that's what you arranged with Sweelinck and his friends, there's no way I could have known that. And if I had known, I really wouldn't have cared, Celia—"

"That's Inspector von du Mark."

"*Deputy* Inspector von du Mark. A bit of free advice: you'd be better off, instead of trying to figure out what I'm going to do and how to mess that up, looking out for yourself. You're not going to catch us violating any of your precious import regs. Besides," I added, just for a bit of misdirection, "if we already did, it's too late."

" 'Not going to catch us.' That sounds as though it would be fairly dangerous for me if I *did* catch you, doesn't it?"

"You're not thinking it through again. Metzada's position is always precarious; I'd hardly take the chance of killing even a Commerce Department *deputy* inspector."

"I saw one of your men eyeing the peacemakers' weapons. So tell me what you'd do if you found that you really needed, say, five wireguns."

"The only thing I could think of is that—given that we really needed five wireguns—it would be kind of convenient if six Commerce Department personnel had been killed in a Dutch ambush. All surviving witnesses would swear to that. The rumors would hurt; witnesses are dangerous."

She started to open her mouth to call for her guard; I silenced her with a quick shake of my head. "Go easy. You've got four deaths on your conscience. Isn't that enough for today?"

Celia gave me a long, slow look. "You might be bluffing. I don't think you'd really kill everyone aboard this boat, just to avoid a beating."

I just smiled. "Would you?"

"No, of course not. I—"

"Would rather take a beating. Which suggests you've never been on the receiving end of a good working-over."

"And you have."

"A few times." I shrugged. "I didn't like it much." I lit another tabstick. "I'm not bluffing, Celia. I can't afford to. Never, Deputy Inspector von du Mark, *never* try me. Metzada has a reputation, the Bar-El clan and its Hanavi family have a reputation . . . and I'm busy building one for myself. Don't try and find out if it's well-founded. Just take my word for it."

"Reputation is worth killing for?"

I smiled, remembering a deserted Kabayle hut on Endu.

"Easy, all. Tetsuo, it's your turn," the Sergeant says.

I nod; he kicks in the frame of the greased-paper window to distract those inside while I go in through the open door, rolling once, then bouncing to my feet.

"All clear," I say. The hut is deserted; the occupants have fled—but not too long ago, certainly not more than a few hours. The rocks from the central fire are still too hot to touch.

There's nobody here, but they've left behind almost everything. The multicolored blankets that they wear and sleep in, cooking pots, even a rack of spears, over against the far wall, away from the door. And not just spears, either. While they've taken all their guns, I find

*a box of cartridges over in the corner. They'd left in one
hell of a hurry if they'd forgotten those.*

*Off in the distance, I can hear the bleating of goats.
They've even left their livestock behind.*

*And then I see it, sitting on a shelf on the far wall: a
wooden doll.*

*It's dressed in khakis and has the chain-circled magen
David insignia on its left shoulder, a single stripe on its
sleeves.*

*The Sergeant laughs. "A fucking demon doll," he says,
as he takes it down from the shelf. "No wonder they
didn't want to hang around and greet us in person."
There hasn't been a Metzadan in this part of Endu for
fifty years.*

*"Well, Private, I think you deserve a promotion." He
pulls a stylus from his pocket and adds another pair of
stripes to the doll's sleeve, and then puts the doll back
on the shelf.*

*"Okay, kill all the animals, smash everything except
the doll, and then we move out. And keep your fucking
eyes open. Next village might not be so easy," the Sergeant says.*

"Perhaps," I said.

Without another word, she walked off.

Thinking, no doubt, black thoughts. Wondering, certainly,
what we had smuggled down to use on the poor, innocent
Dutch.

It can get annoying when someone clever starts wondering,
and just maybe Celia had developed a bit of cleverness in the
past few years. Or maybe I'd lost some.

"Damn." I stared down at the book in the palm of my hand.
It was too much of a risk keeping it around. A pity, that: an
affection for books runs in my family. Still . . .

So I tossed it overboard, and watched it splash into the
Nouveau Loire. Or Neu Hunse. The *Bolivar* steamed away
from the ever-expanding ripples.

What have we smuggled down? Just an idea, Celia.

And a need, of course. People from rich worlds don't understand that. For Metzada, a million credits isn't merely a number on a fiche, but perhaps a shipment of iodine-heavy Endu kelp that will mean that none of my children get goiters.

I walked to our cabin, nodding in passing to Soloveczik, who was on watch outside.

Shimon and the skirmishers were already asleep. Line soldiers learn to get sleep when and where they can.

I stretched out on the bunk, and pillowed the back of my head on my hands. I didn't bother to undress. No need to go through the motions of trying to make myself comfortable; I wouldn't sleep much, or well.

I never do, off Metzada.

CHAPTER SIXTEEN The New Eighteenth

I'd always thought that Colonel Yonaton Davis looked more like a shopkeeper than an officer: he was a short, wide man with only traces of hair on his shiny scalp, an easygoing smile on his broad face, and a slow way of moving.

Was . . . General Yonaton Davis wasn't taller or slimmer than Colonel Davis had been, and he didn't move any faster.

But the smile was gone, and not just from his face. He stood with his feet planted far apart, his back straight, as though he were carrying all two-thousand-plus men of the Eighteenth Regiment on his back. It's a cliché that a general's stars weigh heavily. It's a cliché because it's true.

He was waiting for us on the outskirts of the encampment, his bodyguards spread out along the riverbank, their eyes on the forest. Yonni always believed in general-staff-as-bodyguards. His personal guard consisted of his G-1, G-4, and G-5, their number-two assistants, plus his Logistics officer.

Off in the distance, the smoke from the French colony rose into the sky, muddying the horizon.

"Shimon," he said, smiling. "It's been too long. You need a set of khakis?"

Shimon Bar-El shook his head. "I'm unofficial this time. Just an adviser."

"You can still wear khakis. At least, around me you can." He nodded to a major with a G-2 flash on his shoulder patch. "Take care of it." The general turned to me. "Tetsuo," he said, taking my hand, "it's been a couple of years since our paths have crossed."

I nodded. "The years have a way of adding up."

Just his mouth smiled. "You don't show it."

I matched his light tone. "I'll have you know that my second wife is now officially the fourth-best reconstructive surgeon on Metzada. When she had to rebuild my right side after that Rand mess, she decided to bring back the face of the twenty-year-old she married."

"And how is Suki? And Rachel, too?" he added quickly. You don't ask after one of a man's wives and neglect another.

"Both are fine. As are yours; I brought some letters," I said, reaching into my bag. "Last I heard, Shmuel was doing awfully well. He's got his company."

"Good. Still with the Twentieth?"

I nodded. "You should be proud of your son. All your children are doing well, far as I know," I said. I let that hang in the air. It would have been strictly contrary to protocol for me to ask directly. But, thank God, it wasn't improper for him to answer my unvoiced question.

"When you have the kind of casualties we've been getting, you also get a few field promotions, Tetsuo. Matter of fact, one Benyamin Hanavi of the Bar-El clan has been bumped all the way from private to full corporal. You might see him around camp." He laughed. "If I tried, I swear I could catch him rubbing dirt into his shiny new chevrons, trying to make it look like he's had them for a while." He nodded slowly. "A good boy. I'm thinking about recommending him for officer training." He snorted. "Even if he is a Bar-El."

A good boy. There was a time in our people's history when that phrase didn't refer to a blooded, seventeen-year-old warrior.

"I've got a Commerce Department deputy inspector and five peacemakers cooling their heels back in Marne. She's busy trying to get in to see Montenier, work out some sort of compromise," I said.

"She's just wasting breath. I know Montenier."

I shrugged. "Air's free, here—but I don't want to leave them alone too long. How about you giving me a quick tac briefing, then we head into Marne? I want to meet this Phillipe Montenier."

"I doubt that. Strongly."

"That's my problem, isn't it? The tac briefing, please. You don't expect us to fix everything blindfolded, do you?"

For just a moment, he relaxed. "You've got a way to do it?" he asked, more prayer than question.

There's long been a bit of tension between our Bar-El clan and Davis's Aronis. Shimon's answer didn't do much to relieve it. "Of course," he said. "It just took a little thought. Something we specialize in. You don't think I am stupid like an Aroni, do you?"

Davis didn't rise to the bait. "*How?*"

"With this." He tossed him the implement we'd borrowed from Skirmisher-Sergeant Levin.

"A shovel?" He raised an eyebrow. "A fucking shovel?"

"You're supposed to call it an entrenching tool."

He snorted. "I'm a general. One nice thing about the rank is that I can call a fucking shovel a fucking shovel. Now . . . what are you planning to do with this. Hit the Dutch over the head?"

It took him only a few minutes to tell us. I'd worked out most of it, but Shimon had a few extra wrinkles.

My memory isn't eidetic, but sometimes it is good. I closed my eyes, seeing in front of me once again a shining page of Twain's *Life on the Mississippi.*

The water cuts the alluvial banks of the "lower" river

*into deep horseshoe curves; so deep, indeed, that in some
places if you were to get ashore at one extremity of the
horseshoe and walk across the neck, half or three-quarters
of a mile, you could sit down and rest a couple of hours
while your steamer was coming around the long elbow,
at a speed of ten miles an hour, to take you aboard
again. When the river is rising fast, some scoundrel
whose plantation is back in the country, and therefore
of inferior value, has only to watch his chance, cut a
little gutter across the narrow neck of land some dark
night, and turn the water into it, and in a wonderfully
short time a miracle has happened: to wit, the whole
Mississippi has taken possession of that little ditch, and
placed the countryman's plantation on its bank (quad-
rupling its value), and that other party's formerly valuable plantation finds itself out yonder on a big island;
the old water-course around it will soon shoal up, boats
cannot approach within ten miles of it, and down goes
its value to a fourth of its former worth.*

Smiling broadly, Yonni Davis shook his head. "A typical bit
of Bar-El insanity. How the hell did you think of—? But it
might work. And there'll be one fine butcher's bill to pay, win
or lose."

"This way, perhaps the Eighteenth doesn't have to pay the
bill," Shimon said. "Besides, the sooner the hot part of this is
over, the better. Rivka is going to want to take the Eighteenth
out and put a lower-grade regiment in. There's going to be a
big Neuva contract coming on."

"Oh?"

"Casas are hiring two divisions. Two full divisions. One
armor, one infantry."

Yonni smiled. "We're coming down on the Casa side? Good."

I shrugged. "They're paying the butcher's bill. But forget
that for now. You've got a campaign to settle here. And maybe
we can give a lesson to the French about trying to hire
Metzada for the impossible. Besides, when it comes to butch-

er's bills, it's better to collect than to pay, no?" I lit a tabstick. "And what do you mean, it *might* work? It damn well *better* work," I said calmly, levelly, as though Shimon hadn't just laid it out for me. "I'd better go deal with Montenier."

I turned to Shimon. "You want in on this?"

He shook his head. "Not my cup of tea. I'll stay here and play G-3 for Yonni. I want to work out some of the details on the dispersal."

CHAPTER
SEVENTEEN Port
Marne

I caught a ride into Port Marne on a supply wagon, one of
ten going into town; it's amazing how much food a regiment
can go through.

The horses were fresh and the wagons were empty going
in; the trip only took us about two hours.

Port Marne was a sprawl of whitewashed wooden buildings,
radiating out from the TW Preserve at the center. There's a
certain sameness to reasonably young colony towns on frontier worlds, particularly in how they smell. Part of it is economics: wood is cheaper to build with than stone, at least
until you get a good power technology going. Streets can be
paved later, except for the main thoroughfares. When it's
muddy, wheeled vehicles can slog their way through, pulled
by horses; when it's very muddy, wheeled vehicles can stay off
the side streets.

You find a lot of horses on young worlds. While turbine
engines may churn out tens of thousands of horsepower, they
don't manufacture baby turbine engines. A mare is a very

good device for manufacturing horses—and horses always produce a lot of manure, which is why the streets smell so bad.

"Expecting trouble?" I asked my driver, a fortyish senior private whose name was Bar Giora. He had a flintlock carbine across his lap, and he rode with his eyes more on the greenery to the side of the road than the road itself, which unnerved me. I'm not used to horses—they can keep themselves from going over the side of the road.

"Nah," he said. "But we had couple of Dutch infiltrators here a couple of weeks back. Pays to be careful. Don't worry, Inspector-General, we'll get you into town nice and safe."

"Tetsuo," I said.

"Avram," he said, and then was silent for awhile. "You mind answering a question?"

"Go ahead."

"That's was really *the* Shimon Bar-El? Shimon the Traitor?"

"That's him. My uncle. Why?" I lit a tabstick and offered him one, but he shook his head.

"Never got the habit. 'Why?' Because I find it hard to believe that Yonni is taking his advice, after he sold out on Oroga."

I didn't answer for a while. "He sold out once. Maybe. Doesn't make him any less than what he is."

"And what's that? Meaning no offense."

"None taken." I didn't have an answer, so I just let the question hang in the air. "How long until we're there?"

"Military warehouse is on the outside of town. It'll be another fifteen minutes walk for you to get to Government House."

" 'Best efforts' clause be damned." Phillipe Montenier's eyes flashed. "Three million quid a year for this *merde*? You little piece of Jew filth—if the Dutch swine don't pay my taxes—*my taxes*, I say—then you will *make them pay*. Is that clearly understood? You will *not* allow them to raid our farms."

He paced across the stone floor of the high-ceilinged salon as though he were a caged beast waiting for dinner—whoever that might be. Shakespeare might have been both an anti-

Semitic bastard and a sodomite who favored little boys, but he was right in having one of his characters be wary of the lean and hungry look.

If Montenier's generals had had that same look, we might have been in a different situation, but the three of them, sitting on a couch like the Three Monkeys, were fat and beribboned. The French have always passed out medals like my Aunt Rivka does her tasteless baked goods.

Just sitting still and staying wary took a little effort; even both together, Montenier's two retainers/bodyguards wouldn't have been more than a moment's work, and I've been taught that a decently-trained soldier should be able to go through ten times his weight of Frenchmen like a hot knife through butter.

I know it's just prejudice, but as my Uncle Shimon says, "There's only three things in the universe I utterly despise: frogs, krauts, and bigots."

I didn't like being called a little piece of Jew filth, and I didn't much like Montenier. In other circumstances, I would have enjoyed feeding him his favorite eyeball—after all, I'm only officially a noncombatant.

However, this was neither the time nor the place, and I wasn't likely to find one, and what you'd rather do has little to do with what you can do or what you have to do, not in this life.

Raising an eyebrow, I looked over at Celia. "Would you like to give the peace-pitch now, Inspector? May as well get it over with."

She spent a good half-second swallowing a retort, then launched into the saccharine you-really-ought-to-be-good-boys routine that someone with a strong stomach must teach them at Commerce Department bureaucrat school.

I tuned it out. It wouldn't work. It never works.

Finally, well-oiled machine through she was, Celia ran down. Too many sandy Montenier objections in the gears.

"Enough." I held up a hand. "Seems to me that we're getting nowhere. Monsieur Montenier?"

"Yes?"

"Am I to believe that you doubt that the Eighteenth Regiment is adhering to the best efforts clause?"

For a moment, Gallic temperament threatened to burst a blood vessel, but then, sensing that I wanted him to blow his stack, he forced himself to calm down.

"Yes," he hissed. "Your . . . *regiment* is doing nothing. They are not engaging the Dutch—"

I punched for my command voice. "*Shut up.*" Surprisingly, the flow of sound ceased. "We aren't engaging the Dutch," I went on, "because any movement upriver would leave Marne open to an assault by the Dutch irregulars, and because a Dutch *company* could carve its way through what you idiots call a defense." Not that a Dutch confederate force could destroy the launcher—the peacemakers protecting it wouldn't let them, and the Dutch wouldn't even if they could—or even maintain control of it for long—but a decent-sized Dutch force could leave Port Marne burning.

Which would tend to take the spirit out of the French.

The fattest of the three French generals started to take exception to what I'd said, but I shut him up with a glare.

"So," Montenier said, following the word with another sniff, "you intend to try to fulfill the best efforts clause by having your regiment sit on your hands, *protecting* Port Marne? I'll have your bond forfeit, I swear I will."

I snickered. "Read your contract, Montenier. Forgetting the fact that you can't afford to pay interest on our bond while waiting three, maybe four standard years for a court-date—paragraph twenty-seven, 'Forfeiture of Performance Bond,' subparagraph (j)—the moment you move to seize the bond, the Eighteenth pulls up and heads for home—subparagraph (1)."

Celia smiled slyly. So, she probably thought, that was really what we really were after: pushing Montenier into slapping a lien on the performance bond so that the Eighteenth could withdraw without losing much face.

Not a bad guess, I thought. Just wrong.

Montenier apparently decided the same thing Celia had. "So," he said. "There will be no best efforts payment made, General Hanavi—"

"Inspector-General."

"—and I'll have papers prepared ordering the regiment into combat against the Dutch. They are to assault the Dutch regiment stationed at—"

I shook my head. "Read the contract again. Tactical decisions are General Davis's prerogative, not yours. If you want the Dutch attacked, you'll get it, but—"

"When—and where?"

"—General Davis will decide. The regiment will move out in two days, to give you time to arrange a better defense. As to when and where we'll attack, it's none of your damn business. I'll expect to see written orders or notice of a lien by nightfall."

I turned and walked away, my heels clicking on the stone.

Celia's words echoed after me: "Is this what you do for your money, Tetsuo Hanavi?" And, unspoken, *Do you kill for someone like Montenier?*

No, Celia. Never.

Yonni Davis was in his tent playing bridge with Shimon, a major, and his message runner when I got back to the encampment.

"Well?" Yonni asked.

"Ease up, General. Give the boy time to catch his breath," Shimon said.

"Still babying me, Uncle?" I chuckled. "Orders will be on their way shortly, Yonni. Can you have the Eighteenth ready to move out in two days?"

He nodded. "It can be arranged. Or sooner, if need be."

"Don't rush," Shimon said. "To begin with, you're going to have to break them down to companies, maybe down to platoons, then have everyone sneak upriver about five, six hundred klicks, running a further dispersal all the way. And that's going to take a good forty days, what with slipping through Dutch lines and all."

"They can do it in thirty," he said. "Only question is the provisions caches. I don't like the idea of trusting the captain of the *Bolivar*."

Shimon smiled. "So, you use dried, and you requisition some horses to carry provisions for you. Keep them and the hostlers far enough from the river and your quartermasters won't be spotted." He pulled a map from his pocket and handed it to Yonni.

"Maybe we should try to feel out the captain of the *Bolivar*, instead? I mean—"

"Asshole." Shimon looked at him as though he'd just failed the test. "Whose plan is this? Yours?" He shook his head. "No. It's one of my fixes. I've run into a total of four campaigns, in my whole life, where there was a fix available. You've lucked into one." He'd started to work himself up. "And what does it cost Metzada? An offworld ticket for me?"

"On Thellonee, it cost us Tzvi Hanavi, Yehoshua Bernstein, and Yehudah Nakamura," I said quietly. "It cost us Zev here."

For a moment, his face softened. But just for a moment. "Start thinking like a general. You can always spend one life if it saves two. Three of those lives hardly count, not militarily. Tzvi was only an average teacher; Bernstein and Nakamura were just filling in time, waiting until they died."

He swallowed once, hard. "But they pulled me out of that mess, and if that has any military significance at all for Metzada, it's because I've got a way to shorten this campaign here, to save some lives. So you just shut up and do what you're told, and I'll have a hell of a lot of the new Eighteenth home alive, instead of buried here, dead. End of diatribe." He shrugged. "Over to you two."

Yonni's face was grave. "Very well. Now, what's next?"

"What's next is you get the Eighteenth ready to sneak upriver. Can they do it in forty days?" Shimon unfolded the map. "Trick here is that population is all along the river, near the hempwood. You swing half your regiment east here, half west, have them push maybe fifteen, thirty klicks away from the river itself. They can move north fast—without fear of being spotted—as long as you don't do anything silly. Just send in detachments to pick up supplies."

Yonni nodded. "How about the French?"

"I talked to your G-2. They're on the spots indicated on the map. Keep your skirmishers out in front and you should be able to sneak by."

Yonni looked at it for a long time, then raised his head. "We can do it in thirty days."

"Take forty. The river will be fully swollen in forty days."

"Right." Yonni smiled. "Tetsuo?"

I nodded. "Sounds fair." I rose. "I'm going to go see my son. I won't have another chance, unless you're going to send me out with his company."

"Negative," Yonni said. "I'll want you and Shimon to stay with HQ com—" he caught himself, and smiled. "Make that HQ squad."

I found Benyamin over at his company's campsite, squatting by the fire, checking over his fire team's flintlocks, bows and arrows. The four privates in his fire team, ranging in age from about Benyamin's seventeen to a senior private in his forties, were all watching him more with tolerance than irritation.

His face broke into a smile when he saw me.

It staggered me for a moment. It wasn't his smile. It was the other Benyamin's smile, it was my brother's smile. It wasn't friendly or unfriendly; it was a report: *All is well; I'll take care of everything*, it said.

"Corporal Hanavi," I said, "all's well at home." There is a special spot in hell reserved for people who let others worry for a second longer than necessary.

"Be with you in a moment," he said, as he finished checking the blades of a razorhead arrow, then slipped it back into the quiver, handing the quiver to the bowman it belonged to. "Not bad. Now, if the rest of you get your arrows that sharp, we'll be in better shape next time."

Two of the privates nodded; a third pursed his lips with irritation at the lecture.

The last one, the senior private, said, "Yes, Corporal," and as Benyamin turned away, smiled and nodded at me, his eyes twinkling.

I gripped my son's hand firmly, although I wanted to take him in my arms and hug him the way I used to do when he was younger. But not in front of his fire team.

He hugged me. "It's so good to see you," he said as he pulled away. "Some problem?"

I shook my head. "Just a surprise visit. Your Great-Uncle Shimon wanted to give some information to Yonni."

"That's what we heard," one of the privates called out from around the fire. "He got a fix for us?"

"Shut up. If Yonni wants us to know something he'll tell us," the senior said. "Sorry, Inspector-General," he said, rising and beckoning the others away. "It's getting time for us to be turning in, if that's okay, Corporal."

Benyamin nodded. "Just fine, Yitzhak."

The privates moved away.

"Good men," Benyamin said, then shook his head as though to clear it. "Any news from home?"

I shook my head. "All fine, with one exception. Your Great-Uncle Tzvi died, on Thellonee."

There are limits to our self-control, but we must go beyond those limits. I know that doesn't make sense, but what I did was make quiet chitchat with my son for another few minutes, then I bid him a goodnight and made my way to my own tent, and lay down.

And cried like a baby.

The Sergeant was dead, and I hadn't even had the chance to say goodbye to him.

In the morning we moved out, moving north. Forty days later, we were in position.

CHAPTER
EIGHTEEN Simple
Solutions

Yonni Davis was no Shimon Bar-El; my uncle's kind of genius is rare. Still, he impressed me. There's a reason why generals who are authorized to run low-tech operations on worlds like Alsace, Rand and Indess are generally considered the elite of the elite. On high-tech worlds, reasonably sophisticated comm gear can let a commanding general shortcut down to running a regiment by company, sometimes by platoon, the rest of the chain of command listening in, ready to take over if the enemy takes out either the communication system, or the general.

With sound intelligence and good troops, running a high-tech battle is relatively easy—when you compare it to what Yonni Davis was up against on Alsace. On low-tech worlds, C^3I is never easy. Even in a set-piece meeting engagement, a general has to give up almost all tactical control for everything beyond HQ company—and, more often than not, he has to run most of HQ company as a formation, not a tactical unit; even a loud voice can only carry so far.

And here, Yonni had had to break the Eighteenth down to loosely-linked sections of even more loosely-linked platoons, the whole regiment spread out along hundreds of klicks of riverbank, trusting to his officers and senior enlisted to keep everything quiet and do everything right on the numbers. Particularly the withdrawal. Granted, the Dutch irregular force would soon evaporate, but there was sure to be at least one assault through to Port Marne. The Eighteenth would have to be back, and well dug-in.

All of which explains why I was impressed with the way Yonni's round face was unworried as it gleamed, sweaty in the moonlight. The moon was almost full tonight, and so bright I could have read by its light.

He rubbed at the small of his back as he leaned on his shovel.

His headquarters section was spread out along the bank of the rising river and into the woods, three bowmen posted to watch for any sign of the movement from the farmers in the house less than half a klick away, out on the promontory.

The other thing that stretched out into the woods was a narrow ditch, perhaps a meter wide and half as deep, that cut all the way across the peninsula of the Haugen plantation. Working hard, twenty men could each dig through ten meters of the soft riverside dirt per hour, and we had been at it since just after dark.

One foot in the water, one foot out, I pitched another shovelful onto the waist-high earth dam that was already melting away into the swirling river.

A low whistle was picked up in the distance and echoed, each echo louder and closer.

"Fine," Yonni said. "Signal back: move out. We've got another one to do before morning." He turned to Shimon. "I think you should do the honors."

It only took Shimon a couple of minutes to clear away the dam. The water quietly rushed into the ditch, the newly-made stream rolling off into the night, pulling little morsels of dirt from the edge of the ditch. It almost seemed to grow as we watched. By noon, the rising river would have established the cut-off as a wide wound, growing wider.

Yonni shook his head in amazement. "Are you sure they won't be able to do anything about it?"

Shimon shrugged. "We've been through this before. Nothing."

The Haugens, who lived out on the peninsula that would soon become an island, wouldn't necessarily think that their inland neighbors did it, although perhaps they might suspect them. It wouldn't matter. The news would fly to the Dutch forces in the south. Any of the Haugen sons in the Dutch irregulars would find it hard to fight on behalf of their formerly inland cousins. The inland cousins would find defending their newly-valuable plantation more pressing than fighting the French.

And the scene would be repeated, up and down the river, as the Eighteenth shortened the Neu Hunse this night, putting the ownership of a good portion of Dutch territory into question.

No, it wasn't over. We'd have to get back downriver; surely whoever was commanding the Dutch irregulars would try for one last push before his command collapsed underneath him, and the Eighteenth and the French forces would have to hold the line.

The Eighteenth would hold. Even without the French forces.

And Phillipe Montenier would win, at least in the short run. It would surely take more than the remaining five years of our contract for the Dutch to straighten things out well enough to support a unified fighting force. More likely than not, they'd fragment and end up feuding among themselves for most of a century. The French could play divide and conquer, and their coffers would overflow.

For now. But that was enough. A neat, clean solution.

A shot shattered the silence.

One of Yonni's men pitched forward as leaves rattled to reveal a dark form rising, dropping one flintlock rifle, bringing another to bear.

No orders were issued; none were necessary. A hail of

arrows cut through the darkness, were rewarded by a shrill scream.

I'd already pushed Shimon down, and was covering him with my own body.

"Who the fuck was—?"

"We got that one. Anybody got another target?"

"I got him, I know I got him. Anybody see anything else?"

"Shit, David's hurt bad. Medician, we need the fucking medician over here."

Yonni was down near us, his runner already at his side.

"Message to Lieutenant Goldblatt," he whispered. "Pass up and down the line. From: me. Location: half-klick south of Haugen house, grid—Yisroel, what's the grid? Fine—grid 1353. Text begins: shot fired, one enemy spotted, down. Reconnoiter, and take the Haugen house if advisable. Likely this was an isolated householder, but don't assume; I will advise. Sound retreat if a section-sized or larger force is encountered, or if you get any evidence of such a force. In any case, at 0200 hours or upon receipt of this message, all forces are to begin withdrawal, if they have not already done so. Go." The runner crept off into the night.

"Issur," Yonni snapped out. "This one's yours. Take it. Tetsuo's good on a sneak; use him if you want." The old principle always applies: the person most competent to handle a given situation should be in tactical charge.

"Yes, sir." The lieutenant he'd indicated snapped out a series of orders, ending with: "Inspector-General Hanavi and I will take the point. Cover us."

I became Silence, and crept off into the night.

There were no other attackers, and it wasn't really a householder who had taken the shot at us. It wasn't even, as I'd hoped it would be, a householder's son, too young to go off to the wars.

It was a householder's daughter.

In fifteen minutes, having assured ourselves that there was

nobody else in the immediate area, Issur Pinsky and I were standing over the body of a girl of maybe fifteen.

Just a child, really. I get awfully tired of fighting children.

She was quite dead. Arrows had taken her in the shoulder and chest, and one lucky shot had caught her in the right eye, shoving almost ten centimeters of shaft and blade into her brain.

But she was just a girl, wearing the unisex uniform of a Dutch farmer: a dull gray hempwood-cloth shirt and trousers. A silly thought occurred to me, about how the fabric didn't take dyeing well, and about how that probably meant that you could wash the blood and the piss and the shit out of it fairly easily.

Issur Pinsky pulled her shirt up over her eyes, but that didn't look right, a fifteen-year-old girl lying on the ground with her breasts exposed to the gaze of a couple of bastards like us, so he pulled the shirt back down and turned the body over.

"Just a kid, defending her turf, instead of running. Idiot." He shrugged. "No big deal."

"No big deal," I echoed.

He sighed. "Glad this sort of shit doesn't bother me," he said, as he picked up the girl's flintlocks, his knuckles white around their barrels.

CHAPTER NINETEEN "All the Stars in All the Galaxies . . ."

Alsace, Northern Continent
Somewhere on the Neu Hunse
04/03/44, 0719 local time

Shimon took me aside the next morning, as we were packing up for the trip down south. Our squad had an easy first day; we were scheduled to move only thirty klicks, to a rendezvous, where we'd be joining up with two other squads. Running a dispersal in reverse is even tricker than running the dispersal in the first place; the idea is to get as much of your force concentrated as quickly as possible.

"Got something for you," he said. "Let's take a walk."

"Make it quick, you two," Yonni Davis said. He was already shrugging into his pack. "We're pulling out in fifteen minutes."

"Won't take long," Shimon said.

"I've got something for you," my uncle said, opening a map and handing me a flimsy. "The *Bolivar*'s downriver schedule. If you can make forty klicks a day for the next three days, they have a stop at the Miles Rouper plantation, right here, just about dawn." He smiled. "You're a noncombatant, remember? Just be sure you hide in the trees until they arrive, and then quickly get yourself on board. Now, you'll want to make camp well off the paths—"

"Uncle, I'm not fifteen anymore."

He laughed as he handed the map over. I folded it and put it in my pocket. "So you aren't. Which leaves one bit of unfinished business between you and me. How you're going to explain to Rivka why you didn't kill me."

The words hung there between us.

"You can't do it, Tetsuo," he said. "You should have known that you couldn't, ever since Indess."

"When Yonni took me by surprise."

He snorted. "When Yonni took *you* by surprise? I've got a whole lot of respect for Yonni, but he's a clumsy ox. Even if he wasn't, Tetsuo, I know about your training. That's one of the reasons that Pinhas probably concurred with Rivka: I know too much about a lot. With your training, I bet that nobody can take you by surprise—not if you don't want them to, and certainly not Yonni."

He pulled a pair of tabsticks from his shirt pocket and thumbed them both to life, handing me one.

"You're saying that I wanted to be stopped. You're counting a lot on family loyalty, traitor."

For a moment, his lips whitened, but then he shrugged. "I'm counting on no such thing, Inspector-General. I'm counting on your sense of proportion, Tetsuo."

"You think I have some great sense of proportion?"

"Not at all." His voice softened. He cupped his hands together, then moved them apart, moving them alternately up and down a few centimeters, as though they were the scales of a balance. "You're a barbarian, Tetsuo." He extended his right hand just a little. "Put the welfare of Metzada, of Am Yisroel, on this side, and put the welfare of that girl we killed last night on this side," he said, now pushing his left hand forward. "Which weighs heavier for you? Which is more important to you, Tetsuo Hanavi?"

I shrugged. "Metzada. So?"

"Add the welfare of all of the Dutch of Alsace, and the

French, and then put all of the rest of humanity on the other side of the scales, and which weighs heavier?"

I didn't answer.

"I know, Tetsuo. I know." He shrugged. "Metzada. Our people. Our tribe. A barbarian puts his tribe before all else, Tetsuo, and you are a barbarian. Put all the lives on all the worlds on all the stars in all the galaxies in my left hand, and there's still no contest," he said, a momentary quaver in his voice.

Shimon Bar-El shook his head. "That's why you didn't find my little joke funny. 'This thing that Ruth did, was it good for the Jews?' It isn't funny, because to you that's *precisely* the correct question, the central one, the only one that really counts. Not 'what are my orders' or 'what is the Law' or 'what do I want to do,' but 'is it right for Am Yisroel, is it good for the people of Israel, is it good for the Jews.' No matter how it may seem to others, that's how you make your decisions, Tetsuo Hanavi, that's the scale that you measure everything by."

Shimon Bar-El took a final puff, then ground the tabstick under his heel. "And that's why you won't hurt me, why you can't hurt me," he said, his eyes steady on mine.

"So stop pretending, and go home.

"You can't harm me, Tetsuo, because you know me, and you know what I am, and you know that I couldn't laugh at that joke, either."

PART FOUR METZADA

There was a little city, and few men within it; and there came a great king against it, and besieged it, and built great bulwarks against it. Now, there was found in it a man poor and wise, and he by his wisdom delivered the city; yet no man remembered that same poor man.

—Ecclesiastes 9:14–16

CHAPTER TWENTY "It Doesn't Matter"

Metzada, Bar-El Warrens
Hanavi family quarters
06/12/44, 2012 local time

Just over a thousand hours later, I was back on Metzada, walking down my home tunnel. I waved happily to cousins as I let my feet break into a run for the last klick. Homecoming is a joyous time in the Bar-El warrens; most Bar-El men spend far too much time offplanet.

I always see the children first. If it's daytime—not surface daytime, of course, but the twenty-four hour clock we use, always set to Jerusalem time—I pull them out of school. RHIP.

But it was night.

Rachel knows my habits even better than Suki. The moment I dropped my bag in the foyer, she led me down the hall and into my study. "Suki and I set it up as a nursery while you were offplanet."

I was a little surprised. "Not leaving them in crèche?"

She sort of shrugged. "Not for tonight, not your first night home." She slid the door aside. "Suki'll be home in a couple of hours," she whispered. "She's doing a . . . mandouble reconstruction—"

229

"Mandible," I said. "Mandible."

She squeezed my hand and shook her head for a moment. "Your shuttle was down two hours ago," she said. It was a question.

"I had to see the deputy."

Rivka is furious. I can tell because her voice is flat, emotionless. Pinhas always looks the same; his face is a mirror to his thoughts in exact proportion to his willingness for it to be.

Alon isn't sure; he had a taste of what Shimon's capable of on Thellonee.

"You let him live," she says.

I shrug. "He'll probably go back to Thellonee and set himself back up in a consulting business. He'll be more careful this time—or maybe not. Doesn't matter. I'm sure he's not going to do anything to harm Metzada. Something he said." I shrug.

Pinhas doesn't ask me any questions. He knows better. What would I say?

"I thought it was the right decision," I go on. "We're better off with him alive than with him dead."

"And I'd best either back you up or have you court-martialed?"

"Want to hear my preference?"

Pinhas laughs. "No, no. You might give the wrong answer. We'll let it go again, Tetsuo. Maybe you're right."

"Pinhas . . . ."

"No, Rivka." *He shakes his head.* "You'll have to fire the two of us. Or worse."

Alon finally speaks up. "What did he say to you?"

"He told me a joke." *I purse my lips, then shake my head.* "You wouldn't understand."

Alon isn't disposed to leave it at that, but Rivka sighs, then hands me another indigestible cupcake. "If the Neuva thing wasn't heating up so quickly, I might find you more expendable," she says.

Pinhas shakes his head. "Rivka, he just got home."

*"And he'll be leaving in ten days. I've got some things
I want done on Neuva. Maybe you can even find a way
to get close to the Freiheimer general staff," she says as
she turns to me. "And since it worked so well, I'll give
you a half dozen expendables, again." She raises a hand.
"Not Dov—he's going to Casalingpaesa as your brother's
bodyguard. Can you put another team together in that
time?"*

*I'm already reaching for the phone; punch an already
memorized combination.*

"Menachem Yabotinsky," he says.

*"Tetsuo Hanavi here. Can you find five friends in the
next ten days?"*

"What for?" he asks.

"You care?"

"Nah." He doesn't hesitate. "Old, retired, expendable?"

"Yeah."

*Through the phone, I can barely hear metal tinging
off stone. "Imran and Stern okay for two?"*

"They're fine."

"I'll find you another three. One thing, though."

"Yes?"

"Any chance we get to kill some grown-ups this time?"

"Tetsuo, what is it?" Rachel asked.

"I've got to go away again, in ten days," I said.

"No," she said, her black hair whipping around her face like
Celia's had, when she and her peacemakers had escorted me
into the shuttle at Port Marne. "No, you just—"

"Business," I said.

*"Good work," Celia says, her voice dripping with sar-
casm. "Very, very good. Now the Dutch will start fighting among themselves and the French will walk all over
them. Seventy-five percent taxes? Nonsense—Montenier*

*will probably carve the upper river into French holdings
and turn the Dutch into peons."*
I nod. It's true, of course.

The two youngest children were in their cribs. Devorah was
sound asleep, curled tightly in her blankets.
I let my hand rest against the back of her head for a
moment. I've always wondered why the hair on my children's
heads is so much softer, so much finer than anybody else's.

*"Tetsuo Hanavi, how can you be proud of what you
do for money?" von du Mark asks, sneering. "For filthy
money?"*

Little Shlomo was sleeping restlessly, as though he knew
what his own future held, starting in about fourteen years.
Fourteen years . . . I used to think that was forever.
"Take your time, Shlomo," I whispered. "There's no rush."
"A bit of good news," Rachel whispered. "That new ship-
ment of medicines came in just last week. All of the children's
immunizations are up to date."
"Mmm . . . what came in?"
She shrugged. "First installment from Casalingpaesa," she
said, pronouncing the foreign syllables awkwardly.
No, Celia, nobody ever fights for money.
Still asleep, Shlomo reached out and grasped my forefinger,
gripping it more tightly than his little hand had any right to.
We don't fight for money. We fight, and we kill, and we die,
for the credits that keep Metzada alive. The distinction is
important.
"What did you say?" Rachel asked, wrapping her arms
around my waist as she pressed herself tightly against me.
"Tetsuo, what *is* it?"
I shook my head as Shlomo's grip grew stronger.
"Doesn't matter," I said.

About the Author

JOEL ROSENBERG is the author of the bestselling *Guardians of the Flame* fantasy series, as well as of two science fiction novels, *Ties of Blood and Silver* and *Emil and the Dutchman,* all available in Signet editions. Joel and his wife currently make their home in Minneapolis.

Fabulous Fantasy and Sensational Science Fiction
BY JOEL ROSENBERG